POINT BLANK

DIANE M. CAMPBELL

POINT BLANK

SUBSCRIBE

Subscribers get access to all the latest updates from Diane about new releases, FREE bonus extras, and other behind-the-scenes author stuff!

Visit Diane's **WEBSITE** at dianemcampbell.net

DEDICATION

For all those who recognize a great chasm exists
between where they are and where they long to be.

Here's great news!
You have a trustworthy Savior!
He is ready to intervene for you—though He may
choose to do so in ways you would never anticipate.

I lift up my eyes to the mountains—
where does my help come from?
My help comes from the LORD
The maker of heaven and earth.
(Psalm 121:1-2)

I cry out to God Most High
To God, who vindicates me.
He sends from heaven and saves me,
Rebuking those who hotly pursue me—
God sends forth his love and his faithfulness.
(Psalm 57:2-3)

ONE

A gust of wind nipped my ears, and its chill crept down my spine. Turning my collar up, I shifted position on the cold metal bench. From the moment I'd stepped down from the comfort of the Mountain Motorways Bus, I'd been resisting an eerie sense of familiarity with this desolate highway junction. As if I'd been here before. But that initial sensation had since waned, swallowed up by two hours of sitting in the dark outdoors on an uncomfortable seat.

In every direction the road lay empty and silent. I'd expected the bus stop to be in the middle of town, not out on its lonely edge. The only sign of life was an old gas station across the street with a dingy convenience store, and next to that, a rustic café where I had managed to get a cup of hot cocoa just before they locked up for the night.

I checked my watch—9:36. My connection was twenty minutes late. Apparently, Mountain Motorways didn't worry about being as reliable as the big national bus companies. If my phone's battery hadn't died, I could have called someone to ask about the delay.

I'd gone into the gas station's convenience store an hour ago to use the restroom and shrug off the chill, but I had no intention of going back. Not after the creepy feeling I got from the greasy-looking fellow on duty. I'd found him kneeling in one of the aisles restocking candy bars when I entered. He nodded in the general direction of the lavatory in answer to my question, then rose to his feet as I slipped to the back of the store. His gaze followed me while he worked at a wad of tobacco filling his lower lip.

I expected to buy a snack before leaving as a token for use of the facilities, but the idea faded as I walked out of the bathroom and found him behind the cash register eyeing me as I walked up the aisle.

He ran a hand through his oily hair and looked me over before asking, "Anything else I can do for ya?" His puckered lip stretched with an insinuating smile that made my skin crawl.

That's when I left with neither a word nor a morsel. Only the lingering effect of his gaze that kept me edgy all the way back to the bench.

The same bench where I'd sat waiting ever since. Waiting in the middle of nowhere for a ride to a place I wasn't sure I wanted to be.

My heart skipped at a sudden movement in the periphery of my vision. A moment later, a large black cat sprang up beside me on the bench. He studied my surprise with striking blue eyes.

"Hello." I scooted to give him more room. "You startled me."

The cat continued to stare as if attempting telepathy.

"My name's Penny. And you are—?"

He stepped onto my lap and nestled down with a soft mew.

"Oh, I see. I'm just a warm place to rest. You live around here?"

He closed his eyes to my questions.

I stroked his head, detecting the soft vibration of a purr. "Shouldn't you be at home?"

Home. I was far from my own, and I wondered what Dad would say when I arrived on his doorstep unannounced. At the moment, this whole trip seemed like a dumb idea. We'd rarely spoken in the past year, our relationship strained to the point of near non-existence. Since Mom's death our shared grief had been the only common ground—a terrain of loose, barren soil, slowly eroding until only an empty chasm remained between us.

College provided a diversion I had gladly run to, but now, halfway through my sophomore year, I found my heart aching for comfort. A sense of security … of roots … of home.

Would I be able to find it again with Dad, or was I better off elsewhere? That remained to be seen.

The lights at the gas station flickered briefly and went out, leaving only one street light as evidence this wide spot on the highway even existed. Soon after, a jangle of keys carried across the street in the icy stillness. The station attendant had come outside and was locking the door. Soft footsteps on pavement forced me to chance a furtive glance in his direction. He was coming my way with a large bag of trash in hand.

My heart raced. A harsh metallic creak made me look again. He'd lifted the lid of a bin near the curb on his side of the street to toss the garbage in. He dropped the lid with a creaking crash that jolted my nerves, then paused to stare straight at me, forcing my gaze aside. *Please stay away. Just leave me alone.*

An eternity passed before I heard his footsteps recede. A last glance caught him disappearing down a dark alley between the station and café.

Relieved, I exhaled a long-held breath that hung visible in the frosty air.

The cat stared at me.

"I guess it's just you and me now." I checked my watch again—9:47. Still no traffic on the dim stretch of highway. "Looks like the bus isn't coming. What do you think I should do?"

Kitty blinked, stretched to a stand and hopped to the ground.

I immediately missed his warmth. "Are you going to leave me out in the cold?"

He looked back and mewed. Was it an invitation? As he sauntered down the sidewalk, I realized it didn't matter. I couldn't sit on that bench any longer. It was late, and I needed to find a place to spend the night. Snatching my suitcase, I extended the handle and wheeled it behind me.

A wide slope of scattered shrubs along the walkway rose high enough to hide what lay beyond. After only about half of a block, the cat turned into it, quickly climbing through the wild grass.

"Wait! You never said anything about off-roading."

In moments he had disappeared. What was I thinking trying to follow a black cat in the dark? "Kitty, kitty?" I called in vain.

The edge of a rooftop peeked above the slope, partially obscured by foliage and hardly more than a shadow against the indigo sky. Probably the cat's home. Maybe I could ask to use their phone—explain that Kitty had led me to them.

I looked along the sidewalk for a break to indicate a driveway. Nothing. The bus bench was still visible from where I stood, but I knew better than to go back and sit there all night. After a brief hesitation, I pulled my suitcase through the grass and began dragging it up behind me, weaving through the shrubs and bumping castors over rocks and roots.

As I crested the embankment with panting breaths, the house came into view, a large rough-stone structure with a black mansard roof and foreboding dormers. Tangled ivy climbed its boxy facade, and a chaos of overgrown shrubbery and neglected flower beds encroached either side of a walkway that led to the front entry.

Its imposing framework might have dissolved my courage except for one thing—both the porch light and a lamp behind a curtained window next to it offered a promise of cheering warmth.

Surely, Kitty's owner would let me make a quick phone call.

I descended the hillcrest, crossed an overgrown lawn of winter-dead grass and an old cobbled drive which divided the wide lawn from the front yard. I reached the sidewalk and three steps that marched me up to the small, pillared porch. A tarnished brass plate under the glow of the light said "Wayfarer's Inn" engraved in black script. I looked for a bell, but found only an iron knocker in the middle of the tall, dark-paneled door.

Kitty was nowhere to be seen although I expected he would greet me on the porch. Instead, moments after I tapped, a petite, elderly woman appeared, her eyes peering at me over a pair of wire reading glasses.

Before I could speak, she took hold of my arm. "Finally!" She drew me inside and shut the door. "Whatever has kept you out so late?" Her curly white hair waved in worried disarray as her head bobbed.

My shock must have showed because she didn't wait for an answer.

"Well, at least you're not lost out there somewhere. I wouldn't have any idea where to begin looking."

"For me?" It was all I could think to say.

"Yes indeed, for you. Who else?" She turned and hobbled down the hall toward the back of the house. "I don't get many guests these days, and I guess it's just as well." She turned while I slipped off my muddied shoes. "I have some hot water in the kitchen for tea, if you like. It'll help take some of the chill off."

I paused at the strange quirkiness of the old woman, but relief at being indoors had begun to overrule my hesitance. "Thank you, but I only hoped to use your phone."

"Oh?" Her shoulders drew back. "It's rather late. Who would you be calling?"

I could have protested it was none of her business, but in fact, I didn't know who to call. "Well…" I stammered, thinking. "Perhaps a cab or … a hotel."

"Whatever for? Your room is ready upstairs."

I recalled the brass placard on the porch. Right. An inn. Perhaps she mistook me for a previous guest. I attempted to replace my confusion with a confident smile. "Thank you. I'm glad you have room for me."

She spun around on sensible black pumps. "Come along then. The kettle may already be boiling." With that, she marched through a swinging door at the end of the hall.

I propped my suitcase against an umbrella stand in the corner beside me. A formal parlor was visible through a wide entry to my left. The room overflowed with vintage furniture including the lamp I'd noticed from outside. Timeworn furnishings but tidy. To my right was another wide entrance with its sliding pocket doors drawn shut. Ahead, a dark oak staircase led upstairs on the left side of the passage, its newel post topped with a carved lion's head. Despite its menacing expression, I couldn't resist patting it as I walked down the hall.

"You have a lovely house," I told the woman when I reached the kitchen. Though decades out of date, it was clean and bright. She pointed me toward a vintage dinette at one side of the room and carried a kettle over from the stove.

"That's what you said earlier." She poured my cup and another for herself.

"Earlier?"

"When you first arrived, my dear." She looked at me over her glasses again. "You complimented the house—that is, until you saw the shared bath upstairs. But don't worry. There are no other guests tonight. You'll have it all to yourself."

TWO

Perhaps I hadn't heard the old lady right. Or maybe she was a little off her rocker. I studied her a moment while she fiddled with her tea, attempting to squeeze out the bag against a spoon.

"Excuse me, Mrs…"

"Wilton." She set the teabag aside and pointed a crooked finger at a small covered bowl near the center of the table. "Would you mind passing the sugar?"

"Of course." I complied, then took a sip from my cup. "But Mrs. Wilton, I wasn't here earlier. I've never been upstairs. Perhaps someone else came by?"

"You have a twin, Miss Doyle?"

"No." I paused as a flag popped up in my mind. *She just used my name.* "What I mean is, whoever you spoke with, it wasn't me."

"Oh, don't be silly, my dear. Of course it was you." She spooned a generous measure of sugar into her cup and stirred. "Have you contacted your father yet?"

A tingling sensation washed over me. How did she know all these things? She seemed a harmless old lady—

quite sweet in fact—but this was starting to feel like an episode of *The Twilight Zone.*

"Not yet." I managed another sip of tea.

"I thought you were going to let him know you're on your way home."

It was true I had thought about calling ahead, but how did she know? My heart thumped in my chest. Did she also know I'd brushed him off the week before the holidays, telling him I had other things I'd rather do than come home? Did she know about the heart-rending break I heard in his voice when he wished me a Merry Christmas? How it had resounded in my head ever since?

I bit my lip, deciding how best to change the subject. "Mrs. Wilton, could you tell me when the next bus will come? I don't want to miss it."

"Oh…" Her voice held a note of concern. "The bus doesn't stop here anymore."

"But I've been waiting out at the bench all evening. There was supposed to be a bus shortly after nine o'clock, but it never came."

"That's the old stop. The bus goes through to Barrett these days."

"This isn't Barrett?"

"No, no. This is Dalton. Barrett's another thirty-five miles."

"Oh!" Relief settled my shoulders and I set my cup down. "I asked the bus driver to stop because I thought *this* was Barrett. Now it all makes sense." Well, maybe not all of it, but I definitely felt better. My heart rate eased back to normal. "So, do you think I could get the bus to pick me up here when it comes through again, or will I need to find another way?"

"I suppose you can call the station in the morning and ask." She pointed at my cup. "In the meantime, how's the tea?"

"It's wonderful. Thank you. I don't know what I would have done if your sweet kitty hadn't led me here."

Mrs. Wilton's eyebrows rose over the rims of her glasses. "My dear," she said after setting her cup down, "You really think a cat led you here? I'd be much more inclined to consider it the guidance of the Almighty."

"You mean God?" I took another quick sip from my cup. "Sure. I suppose that could be." I said it only to be agreeable, and the tilt of her eyebrows told me she knew it.

A moment later she turned the subject. "Besides, I don't even have a cat."

Suddenly, the entire conversation felt oddly familiar, as if Mrs. Wilton could be right about me being here earlier. I'd had this conversation before. I was positive. I pulled my bottom lip between my teeth, resisting the notion. Déjà vu is merely a neurological delay—nothing more. Still, the sensation lingered. "In any case, I'm here and somehow, you were already expecting me."

Her thumb traced the rim of the cup. "Still sounds like the hand of God to me, Miss Doyle."

I sat back in my chair unconvinced and tried again to move away from the subject. "Please, call me Penny."

She smiled with a twinkle in her gray-blue eyes. "Such a darling name, and it matches your lovely copper-colored hair."

Self-consciously, I smoothed the unruly curls at the nape of my neck. "It's actually Penelope, but I've never cared for it. Penny suits me better."

"So it does."

I finished the tea and Mrs. Wilton guided me upstairs. The effort of hefting my suitcase up to the second floor landing revealed a shoulder pain I hadn't noticed before. I thanked her and she left while I massaged the ache and surveyed the room. It was small but homey, and the bed felt comfortable enough. A window faced toward the back of the property, though it was too dark to see anything. I closed the drapes and pulled my phone from the side pocket of my suitcase. After plugging it into the wall, I retrieved my pajamas and lay them on the bed. While spreading out a fresh change of clothes for the morning, I heard my phone chime. Five text messages and two voicemails.

I scanned the texts. Two were from friends in my chemistry class, acknowledging my earlier message about missing our planned study sessions during the semester break.

Another from my dorm roommate mentioned a visit from my boyfriend: BROCK WAS HERE LOOKING FOR YOU. SEEMS MIFFED. HOPE YOU'RE OKAY.

The other two were from Brock. The first held no hint of the attitude my roomie had reported: HEY, BABE, WHAT'S UP? CHERI SAYS YOU LEFT CAMPUS. The other, sent a couple hours later, was another matter: FIRST YOU DON'T ANSWER MY CALLS AND NOW NO TEXTS? ARE YOU UPSET ABOUT TUESDAY?

I stared at the screen, my mind a blank. What happened on Tuesday? Oh yes, the New Year's Eve party.

We had gone to Tyler's house, a place his parents had rented for him in some gated community off campus. I'd only met Tyler a few times, but he and Brock were practically inseparable.

What *upset* could Brock be referring to? I hardly remembered the party, only that we danced a bit and listened to Tyler rehash highlights of the Panthers championship. Football. A subject he and Brock never tired of. As a diversion, I'd chatted with a couple girls, but the evening had been uneventful. Did we even stick around for the midnight countdown? If so, I didn't remember it.

It was just a party, and a rather lame one at that. Why did he think I was upset?

The voicemails were both from Brock, but I was too tired to care. Besides, it was late. They could wait until tomorrow when the phone was recharged.

While undressing, I caught a glimpse in the mirror of a bruise on the back of my shoulder in shades of deep purple. I massaged it gingerly with my fingers, sensing tenderness deep in the muscle tissues. Clearly, I'd injured it within the last few days, but I had no memory of it. Only a vague sense of unease at drawing a blank.

What happened to me?

THREE

An annoying buzz drew Lance Doyle from the deep comfort of sleep. He caught hold of the bedding and dragged it aside to sit up and study the clock. It silently displayed 1:24 a.m.

The annoying sound repeated nearby in the dark where his phone also vibrated with a soft glow on its face. Was he on call? No. He grabbed the phone and swiped a finger against the screen just below the ID which read: Mercy Hospital ER.

"Hello?" His tone didn't completely hide his annoyance.

"Dr. Doyle, I'm sorry to wake you."

He didn't recognize the girl's voice, but that wasn't surprising. He hadn't worked in the Emergency Department for at least a year. He scrubbed his scalp to chase away the cobwebs of sleep. "Well, you've got me up. What's this about?"

"There's been a wreck out on Highway 16. A bus has rolled over on Granite Pass. Sierra Memorial in Wakeville can't take them all, so they're sending some patients here. Dr. Farthing said to bring you in."

A bus wreck. He stretched his back. "Do you know how many?"

"I think they said eighteen total. Sierra's taking the most critical, but ten or eleven are on their way here. A couple of them are expected to be critical but stable. They need extra hands in surgery."

"All right. Tell Farthing I'm on my way."

"Sorry again, Doctor."

"Me too."

He hung up and switched on the lamp, casting the room in sepia-toned light. If Marla were still here, he would tiptoe around in the dark, trying not to wake her. Not that he had ever been very successful at it. Too often, he'd stub his toe on the bedpost, and then she'd be up, shaking her head and cooing over his pain.

Tiptoeing wasn't necessary these days. Not since cancer took her away. He pressed a hand to his chest at the now-familiar ache that rose with every thought of her loss. The fact that life had gone on without her remained an injury he could not fix. Instead, he'd learned to push back against the tearing wound, especially when he woke during the night.

Lance stood and hurried to get dressed. At least he didn't need to stumble around in the dark anymore. He hadn't stubbed his toe in four years.

In the bathroom, he splashed water on his face and stared into the mirror. Two hours of sleep wasn't enough to get by on, but he'd have to manage. After a quick tooth-brushing, he felt better. He combed his hair and tied his shoes.

Within minutes, he strode into the garage, fumbling in the cold for car keys in his coat pocket. A veil of icy mist hung in the light of the streetlamp. Up on that mountain pass, it would be much worse, with deep snow hampering the efforts of rescuers.

A silent prayer formed in his mind as he got in the car and headed out.

Bright lights and urgent voices filled Mercy Hospital's Emergency Department as Lance entered through the automatic doors. No sign of the ambulances yet. Hurrying to the nurse's station, he found Shenan Hastings rifling through a stack of papers, and shaking her head hard enough to dislodge her tangled bun of micro braids.

She called toward the back room. "No, it's not in here, Liz. You better check again, and while you're at it, talk to Colten about the bloodwork. We're gonna—" She looked up as Lance approached. "Well, there you are. What took you so long?" Shenan's mock chiding, as always, was accompanied by a smile of perfect white teeth contrasting with her mocha complexion.

"Shenandoah Hastings. What has it been—maybe eight months since we worked the same shift?"

"Welcome back to the Dark Side." She chuckled at her term for the night shift, then refocused to the business at hand. "I'm sorry we had to call for you. I bet you were just settling into a nice deep sleep cycle when the phone rang."

Lance shrugged. "Isn't that how it always goes?"

"Sure seems that way. Hopefully, we can relieve you in a few hours, but until then, I'm glad you're here. They've radioed in three head traumas, a couple cases of internal bleeding, and multiple fractures. We're handling the minor injuries here too."

"How much time do we have?"

She checked her watch. "I'm expecting the first of our patients to arrive any minute now."

He jogged to the locker room to prep and then grabbed his lab coat and stethoscope. An ambulance's colored lights were flashing through the front windows by the time he came back up the hall. The first two gurneys wheeled into the triage area, where Shenan and another nurse waited.

Time to get to work.

Back-to-back procedures kept Lance focused through the night. Five hours flew by, and when the last was finally finished, he emerged from the surgical ward and swiped the cap from his head, thoroughly depleted.

A nurse entering the ward gave his arm a quick congratulatory pat as she passed by. "Excellent work, tonight," she said and continued on her way.

Lance nodded and massaged his temples a moment before drawing his fingertips across his dry, fatigued eyes to the bridge of his nose. What a night.

His first surgery had been a young woman with a punctured rental artery, and her family had arrived near the end of her surgery. She wasn't out of the woods yet and would likely remain in a coma for the next twenty-four hours under close observation.

The next patient had a ruptured spleen. Lance was hopeful for a good outcome, as long as the next few hours went well. His third patient was a nine-year old girl traveling with her family. She had a hip dislocation and fracture, but had arrived alert and in better spirits than her overwrought parents.

On first seeing her, the child had reminded him of his own daughter when she was about that age. Penny had broken her leg while they were on a skiing weekend at Breckenridge. Marla had worked herself into a near panic before the ambulance arrived. Penny, on the other hand, already showed her strong independent streak—a quality further developed during the years after her mother's passing.

He crossed in front of an empty waiting room, not a surprise since most of the bus passengers were far from home. Although families had been notified, only a few had arrived. That would change tomorrow.

Then he noticed a window in the corridor framing a view of winter's pink dawn on the horizon. Correction. Tomorrow was already here. Perhaps he should stick around until his patients' relatives arrived. He could catch a nap in his office and have a nurse call when he was needed.

But first things first. Reports needed to be dictated.

He continued up the hall, his paper-covered shoes shushing each tired step.

"Lance," Shenan's voice called from a side door behind him. "Good work. Thanks for coming in."

Only Shenan could sound so chipper after such a long night.

Lance pivoted to face her. "No problem."

"I wanted you to know that Dr. Holloway is here to relieve you."

"Good. I still have some charting to do."

Shenan stepped out of the doorway and put her hand on her hip. "Okay, but after that you go home. I saw Liz updating files, so she may have already recorded most of what you need."

That was no surprise. Liz was always efficient. He smiled and waved as he resumed his walk.

Shenan piped up, "I'm serious, Lance. Go home."

She was right. Others could speak to the families as they arrived, and he would see them later, after he rested. "Yes, ma'am," he called over his shoulder.

The elevator took him up two floors to his office in the east wing. Once behind his desk, he eased into the swivel chair with a sigh, and leaned side-to-side to stretch his lower back. He logged onto the hospital system and searched for the files Liz had started. While scanning the list, he rotated a kink from his neck and worked the muscles with his fingertips.

Clicking open the file from his spleen patient, he began to read, then pushed back into the cushioned black leather to relax his spine. He stretched his legs out under the desk. Dr. Farthing had been right when he recommended this chair.

He yawned. Liz's notes were out of focus to his tired eyes, even with the oversized monitor.

A half hour later, he woke when Shenan tapped on his door.

"Now, what did I tell you?" Her brows arched over piercing brown eyes.

"Yeah, yeah." He groaned and pulled himself up from the chair. "I'm outa here." *And back to my lifeless house.*

"Uh-huh." Shenan nodded as she followed him out of the office.

FOUR

While basking in a hot morning shower I noticed another bruise. *What's going on here?* I strained to examine the discoloration on my right hip while rivulets of soapy water streamed down my skin. Pressing fingers around the edges, I sensed tenderness deep in the muscle. Like my shoulder, it was dark purple—a recent injury. *I should be able to remember how this happened.*

I finished rinsing my hair though my shoulder ache protested the effort. The two injuries must be connected.

After wiping steam from the bathroom mirror, puffy eyes stared back at me. Why did I look as if I'd cried myself to sleep? Maybe it was all those long miles I'd spent on the bus. I dabbed at the bulges with a cool washcloth and then dug around in my makeup kit. Fortunately, cosmetics can hide a multitude of problems.

After blow-drying my hair and snugging into fresh jeans and a warm fleece top, smells of sausage and coffee drew me downstairs. I let my hand slide along the dark, polished handrail and patted the lion head at its base. The old lady's mansion felt less gothic in morning light, its furnishings gaining a bit of faded charm. A little fresh paint on the walls might be enough to draw more guests, not that the success of her business concerned me. Today, I would find a way out of this Podunk town and get back on track for the final leg of my journey.

The parlor beckoned from the base of the staircase. The draperies had been drawn aside to let morning light filter through lacy sheers, casting soft scattered beams over the room.

Behind the parlor's faded green sofa, a wide arch opened to a formal dining area with a large oval table and vintage floral wallpaper. I headed in that direction just as Mrs. Wilton popped through a side door that apparently connected to the kitchen. She carried a pitcher and hummed to herself until my presence caught her attention.

"Ah, Miss Doyle." Her eyes twinkled behind her glasses. "I hope you like grapefruit juice. It's all I have at present. Juice-wise, that is. There's coffee right here—" She indicated a thermal pot on the table. "—or perhaps you would prefer tea or milk?"

"Thank you, Mrs. Wilton, I don't want to be a bother. The juice sounds great, and I've been eager for the coffee ever since the aroma reached me upstairs."

The old woman poured juice while I pulled out a chair. Delicate antique china adorned the table, the kind most people keep on display but never actually use. A small floral centerpiece graced the center of the table. "Everything's so lovely, Mrs. Wilton."

"Thank you. Have a seat, and I'll bring your breakfast." She returned to the kitchen but was back again by the time

I'd poured my coffee. The vintage porcelain held a steaming wedge of some type of egg, sausage and potato concoction. A toasted English muffin perched on its decorative rim. "It's a Dutch Omelet," she said, setting the plate in front of me.

The aroma was heavenly. "I hope you'll join me. I'd like the company."

"I'd love to. I've eaten already, but I'll bring in my tea. Please don't wait. Eat while it's hot."

I took a bite and savored it while I buttered the muffin. "How long have you been doing this?" I asked, when she returned with her tea.

"Oh, I've never kept track of that sort of thing." She sat in an adjacent chair and smoothed out a wrinkle on the tablecloth before setting her cup down. "Seems as though I've been serving the Lord for about as long as I can remember."

"I mean this inn. Have you been here long?"

"Not really. I just go when and where the Lord sends me."

"Hmmm." I nodded, my mouth full.

She seemed to study me for a moment. "You've kept yourself away from home quite a while now, Penny." Her dainty fingers played at a small brooch near her collar. "Do you know why the Lord is sending you back?"

I swallowed and wiped my mouth with a napkin. She spoke as though she'd always known me, which was unnerving enough without hearing everything filtered through her religious bias. I considered a gentle way to answer. "Actually, I think I made up my own mind about returning. If God has an opinion about it, He hasn't let me know."

"Would you like to know what He's told me?" Her expression remained as natural as if she'd asked about refilling my coffee.

I stopped chewing and swallowed hard. "You really believe God talks to you."

"Oh yes, most certainly."

"Well…" I searched my mind for a suitable answer. "I don't think I've ever heard Him. If He has something to tell me, He should probably just say it." I took another bite of the omelet. "Sorry, I hope my opinion doesn't upset you, Mrs. Wilton."

"Not at all. Everyone's entitled to an opinion." She sipped her tea. "I've discovered, though, that many people say they want to hear from God, but then they ignore Him when He makes His wishes known."

I acknowledged the comment with a nod, but kept chewing. "Yummy sausage," I said after a sip of coffee and swallowing. "You'll have to write out the recipe for me."

"Of course, dear, if you like. But I still wonder, would you like to know what God has told me?"

I wiped my mouth with the napkin. "About what again?"

"The reason for your trip home."

I sat back and considered how kind she had been since I arrived. There was no harm in listening. "All right. What has He told you?"

"I believe He has three words for you to consider: Remember, repent, and restore."

I had expected her to come up with something profound—some truism I could nod and smile over. Not three cryptic words. What did she expect me to do with that? Still, I had to admit that a memory boost might be helpful. "Oh … okay. I'll … keep that in mind then." Having finished, I laid my napkin aside and pushed away from the table. "You're a marvelous cook, Mrs. Wilton. Thank you so much for the wonderful breakfast."

She watched me rise from the table without a word, only a look of sadness in her eyes. Or maybe it was concern. I couldn't tell.

"What time do I need to checkout? I feel like taking a walk this morning, and I still need to repack my suitcase."

"Oh?" Her eyes widened. "You're not going to stay another night? You already paid for two."

Already paid? Although she was kind, the poor old woman was also rather batty. "I only have another week before classes resume. I need to get back on the road today."

She stood and began stacking the dishes. "Of course, if that's what you wish. I know your father will be very glad to see you."

Though I wasn't so optimistic about my impending visit with Dad, I didn't counter. Easier to agree than explain my own expectations.

When I returned to my room upstairs, my phone chimed with a new text from Cheri: You home yet? How's it going? Be glad you're not here. Brock was having fits.

Fits? Why? Because I left town without giving him

notice? I replied: GOT STUCK IN NOWHEREVILLE LAST NIGHT. HOME TOMORROW. WISH ME LUCK. TELL BROCK TO CHILL.

Then I remembered the voicemails Brock had left, so I grabbed my coat, went downstairs and out the front door with my phone.

Bright morning sun had cleared the overnight frost and the crisp air was invigorating. I crossed the yard the same way I'd arrived and soon reached the edge of the sloping embankment. In daylight, the elevation afforded an extended view of the community.

Dalton appeared to consist of a few random residential streets meandering behind one block of nondescript storefronts facing the highway. Passersby might overlook it if it weren't for the surrounding peaks that lent it some picturesque charm. I couldn't help drawing a deep breath of Rocky Mountain air and reveling in the sunshine and deep blue skies.

Mrs. Wilton's inn sat isolated on a large property dotted with old trees and overgrown shrubbery. The high embankment where I stood stretched along the highway with the road gradually rising to meet its level at the far end. I looked for a signpost but saw nothing to indicate Mrs. Wilton was officially in business. No wonder she didn't have many guests.

Rather than descend the slope I'd climbed last night, I followed the long cobbled driveway to the far end of the property. My bruised hip would protest against jogging, but a walk around the community would do me good and give me a chance to listen to Brock's messages.

The first was from mid-afternoon yesterday. "Hey,

Penny. So, I hear you decided to go visit your dad. Seems kind of sudden. I just thought I'd check and make sure everything's okay. I know you haven't talked to him in ages." He paused, as if gauging what to say next. "Maybe you'd rather not talk about Tuesday night..." Another pause. "And if so, that's okay. I just wanted you to know I love you, babe. I'm here for ya."

An automated tone separated this from the next message, sent several hours later. The background noise sounded like the gym where he worked. "I'm taking some time off from Rico's after I finish my shift tonight so I can come see you. Don't know how far I'll drive tonight, but I'll call tomorrow to figure out where we can meet up. Can't wait to see ya, babe. Later!"

I shook my head and disconnected. Cheri had said he was having "fits," but he sounded fine. The whole deal about Tuesday was still a mystery, but the fact he would drive hundreds of miles to join me was sweet. Like something from a romantic movie. In fact, since he was coming, I could forget about the slowpoke bus. We could drive together over the scenic mountain passes instead. I could point out favorite spots along the way, and we could hold hands and have each other all to ourselves. No football. No talk about talent scouts and going pro.

Just us. All the way ... home.

Suddenly, I visualized Brock standing beside me at Dad's front door and felt a twinge in my gut. My hand was at the doorbell, but I hesitated. Was it too soon to introduce my boyfriend? Or did this awkward feeling come from avoiding Dad for so long?

Shaking off the vision, I picked up my pace and crossed the highway to Dalton's residential streets. Maybe I should call and let Dad know I was on my way. Lifting my phone, I found his number on the contact list. My pace slowed again as I pondered what to say.

Hi, Dad. I'm on my way for a visit. My boyfriend is with me. Wait, he would think it was serious. *No, Dad I'm not getting married. He's just...* Just what? Handsome and popular? Easy to be with—unlike you?

I cringed and exited the screen. Talking to Dad had never been easy, but it seemed so much harder after Mom was gone. And now that I'd been away so long, it had become even more difficult. Brock's presence would add yet another complication.

Not that Brock was difficult. At least, not most of the time.

My roommate, Cheri, would disagree. She thought Brock was too moody. He had plenty of moments when he wasn't easy to be around, but he was also under a lot of pressure, especially since he was being eyed for the upcoming NFL draft. Cheri didn't know him as well as I did. She hadn't seen his quirky humor, or heard how passionate he was about team loyalty and commitment, both of which were qualities to admire.

Would Dad be able to see what I saw in him?

Cheri also criticized the pressure Brock put on our relationship. She didn't see how he challenged us to be a better couple. He took life seriously and had high expectations. Perhaps Cheri's opinion would improve when she saw how much Brock missed me and how he made this long drive to be with me.

I tucked the phone in my pocket and tried a brisker walking pace. This would be the first time Brock and I spent together outside the context of school and his game schedule. It could turn out to be positive for both of us.

Once again I tried to visualize Brock standing with me at Dad's door, but when it opened, Dad's expression was an indiscernible muddle.

I sighed. My thoughts about Dad had become a lot like my thoughts about Mom. For different reasons, both of them made my heart ache. If I hadn't gotten off the bus last night, I would be there already. I'd be standing at the front door, mustering the courage to face the gulf between us. I hoped that, with Brock coming, he could help me figure things out. Help smooth the awkward transition back home.

With any luck, this detour in Nowhereville would turn out to be a blessing in disguise.

FIVE

After wandering on a loop that took me on every dusty street in town, I returned to the main road and decided to stop in at the café. I stepped up onto the boardwalk porch and caught sight of a carved, hand-painted sign over the door, as weathered and faded as the rest of the building. It read *Café Du Louvre* in embellished script. A suitably humorous name, given that I'd noticed the walls were covered in artwork for sale when I picked up my cocoa last night.

The bell jangled as I entered, and some old farmer-types in a corner booth glanced my way. An older couple stood at the cash register. The waitress looked up while handing them change. "Have a seat. I'll be right with you."

I found a small table by the front window and scanned the menu card decorated with hand-flourished script similar to the sign outside. "You'll 'louvre' our pie!" it cheerfully proclaimed under clear laminate.

The waitress brought a glass of water to my table. She seemed about my age, with brown hair pulled back into a ponytail. Her name badge read *Cassie*. "I see you've noticed my parents' lame sense of humor," she said.

"And their artistic flair," I added, with a pointed glance around the room.

"You mean the paintings? That's my mom's department, but we also consign stuff for others sometimes. There are folks with some genuine talent around here."

I nodded toward a wildlife scene nearby. "Your mom's very talented, and I appreciate her lame humor too."

"Fortunately, the pie here *is* really good," She pulled a notepad from her apron and swept her bangs aside with the clicker end of her pen. "It's just the jokes that are lame."

I looked at the menu while twisting my mouth. "It's tempting but … pie in the morning?"

"I can get you some breakfast instead. What do you like?"

"Well, I ate breakfast a couple hours ago…"

She crouched next to me and looked around conspiratorially. "If you really want the pie, I say, go for it. Like my dad says, 'Life is uncertain. Eat dessert first.'"

I played along. "A wise man, your father. Got some coconut cream?"

"Comin' right up!"

My phone rang soon after she bounded away.

Brock.

"Hi!" I set the menu aside. "I was just about to call you. I didn't get your messages until late last night."

"I've been worried about you." His voice sounded controlled, as if hiding an underlying annoyance.

"Sorry. The phone battery was dead yesterday, and I was tired when I finally got a room for the night."

"So, out of the blue, you decided to go visit your dad and you didn't think about talking to me? Did you forget we had plans for the *Wreckless* concert on Friday?"

Oops. He and Tyler had discussed it before the New Year's party. "Sorry. You're right. I forgot."

"Sorry? That's all? It's a good thing I hadn't bought the tickets yet."

"Sorry." I bit my lip, realizing I'd said it again.

"I just wish you hadn't left like you did. You had me worried."

"But there's nothing to worry about." A chill made me grasp my shoulder with my free hand, raising the ache of my bruise. "I've been missing my dad, that's all."

"I thought you were glad to be away from him. Is something bothering you?"

"No." *Just my faulty memory.*

"Well, that's good to hear. I left Phoenix about three hours ago and stopped to get something to eat."

"Why such a late start?"

"I had to take care of some things with Tyler after I got off work. It took a lot longer than I hoped. So where are you, anyway?"

I bit my thumbnail. "I'm not at my dad's yet. I messed up and got stuck in some little town thirty miles from my connection. It's called Dalton."

"How far is it from your dad's?"

"I'm not sure. Maybe hundred miles over a couple mountain passes. I was supposed to catch a bus out of

Barrett. It would have gotten me home at twelve-thirty or one a.m." I took a sip of water, wishing my stomach would relax.

"One o'clock? What were you going to do? Ring his doorbell in the middle of the night? Does he even know you're coming?"

Brock made it sound like a dumb idea. Like I hadn't thought things through. "I haven't talked to him yet. I figured I would get a room somewhere and then let him know I was in town."

"Well, the good news is I should be able to get to you late tonight and then we can drive the rest of the way tomorrow and see him together."

Again, I imagined Brock standing with me at Dad's front door. Awkward and uncomfortable were two words that sprang to mind. Could I ask him to wait in the car? Conflicting thoughts jumbled in my head. He was waiting for an answer, so I finally conceded. "Sure. I guess maybe we could do that."

"Maybe? Gee, Penny, I'm trying to help, since you haven't seen him in a long time. You sound like you're scared of him or something."

Was that the reason my gut was churning?

Brock's voice softened again. "I want to be there to support you, babe."

There was no point arguing. "Sure. Okay. And sorry again about the concert."

Brock sighed. "This is important too. There'll be other concerts. See you tonight."

I ended the call and stared at my water glass.

A moment later, Cassie brought the pie. "Here you go."

"Thanks." I offered a smile, though I no longer felt like eating. "Actually, could you bring me a box for it?"

"Everything okay?" She tilted her head, her eyebrows raised.

"Yeah. My boyfriend is driving up today to see me."

"And … you're not happy about that?"

I opened my mouth to protest, but it seemed she might be right. "Maybe. I don't know yet."

After taking care of the check, I stepped outside into the sunshine. A loud rattle of power tools drew me to the end of the café's front porch. Across the alley, in the open garage of the gas station, someone lay on the concrete his head and torso under a dark-colored sedan with its hood raised. I couldn't see if he was last night's lecherous tobacco-chewer or not.

My attention was drawn to the mechanic's boots sticking out from under the vehicle. I set the pie box on the porch railing and my hand brushed against the weathered wood. A sudden dizziness overcame me. Shifting shadows blurred my vision, and I grasped the top rail. As if through a tunnel, I had a vision of someone else lying on concrete— someone without boots or shoes.

My heart pounded in my ears.

Bare feet—concrete.

The darkness shifted again and pain shot through my hip as the scene swirled and tumbled.

"Oh!" I clenched the railing and leaned over it for support. Then the morning sun pushed the swirling shadows from my mind. Noises from the garage resumed, and I found myself blinking at the flower bed below the porch.

What just happened? I grasped for the fading mental image of those feet on the concrete slab and took a deep breath. I turned my back to the railing as the dizziness faded.

Birds chirped. A car drove by on the highway. The second story of Mrs. Wilton's inn was visible across the street. Like the sensations of déjà vu that seemed to strike at random, this too was a mystery.

With a shake of my head, I picked up the Styrofoam container and stepped off the porch. Time to head back.

My phone rang as I crossed the highway and my roommate's photo appeared on the screen.

"Finally! You answered!" Cheri's voice oozed with exaggerated desperation.

"Sorry. I didn't know you were trying to get ahold of me." *Seems like apologizing is all I do.*

"That's okay. I suppose service is sketchy up there in the mountains. Have you heard about Abbi Maxwell yet?"

"No." The name sounded familiar. "Who is she?"

"You know, Tyler's girlfriend. I'm sure you saw her at the New Year's Eve party."

"Oh yeah, I remember her." *The one I tried to ignore.*

"The party is the last time anyone has seen her."

I stopped midstride. "What? She's missing?"

"They've been hunting for her since yesterday, or maybe the day before. Anyway, with you being one of the last people who saw her, the cops want to talk with you."

"Me? I don't know anything."

"I told them that's what you'd say."

"You talked to the police?"

"They came here looking for you. Then Brock came by and interrogated me about it. They spoke with him too. I suppose they interviewed everyone who was there that night."

"Well, I don't know anything about it." Fact was, I barely remembered the party.

"I figured." She paused a moment. "It's weird, huh? You hear about people disappearing sometimes, but you never expect to *know* someone who does."

I stepped onto the sidewalk and a car passed behind me. "I bet that's why Brock was having fits." I might too, if I'd been questioned by the police.

"Yeah, he was pretty riled up about it—and about you leaving town."

"Don't worry. I talked to him and everything's fine now." Maybe not entirely, but it would be soon. "He's coming here so we can go the rest of the way to my dad's house together. We'll be back by the time classes resume."

"Well, I don't know if this stuff about Abbi's disappearance should change your plans or not, but you should probably call the investigator and tell them anything you know."

"Which is nothing."

"Maybe. They left a card here. I'll text you the number."

Cheri couldn't see my eye-roll, but I did it anyway. "Okay."

I ended the call and continued back to the inn. It was

weird that Brock didn't mention anything to me about Tyler's missing girlfriend. Not one word. Especially since it was probably the biggest news on campus right now. Maybe he planned to outline all the sordid details of his police interrogation in person.

I took a deep breath and continued up the hill to Mrs. Wilton's cobbled driveway while massaging my aching shoulder. The bruise may have started with some unbeknown injury, but at the moment it felt like the extension of a much larger uneasy sensation trying to take hold of every other part of me.

SIX

Lance poured milk on his mid-afternoon breakfast while details of the bus crash headlined the NetNews video report on his tablet. "One fatality has been reported so far in the late night rollover on Highway 16 south of Wakeville..." The report droned in the background while he checked his phone for messages. Nothing. Surely, family members of the injured had begun to arrive by now, but he hadn't gotten any phone calls since he got home. Shenan must have told the staff to let him sleep.

The report shifted to video clips captured at the scene. Lance paused chewing to lean toward the small screen. Much of the camera view was dark, with glimpses of flashing emergency lights and recovery crews hauling stretchers up a steep embankment. A shot showing the condition of the bus made him wince and appreciate the miracle that so many had escaped serious injury.

He finished eating while making calls. First to his office, which confirmed his afternoon appointments had been covered. Then he checked in with the hospital. His call went straight to the charge nurse at the ICU.

"The family of your spleen patient got here a couple hours ago," Jill said. "I think Dr. Farthing is available to review the boy's chart with them, if you like."

"No need. I'm almost ready to head back in now. You can let the family know I'll be there soon." He hung up, finished dressing, and grabbed his shaver as he went out the door.

When he arrived at the ICU, he found Dr. Farthing standing in front of the nurse's station, studying a computer tablet.

"I'm glad you're here." Farthing passed him the screen. "I was looking over your young man's chart to see what encouragement I could offer his family."

"Jill let me know his folks arrived. That's why I'm here. I appreciate your willingness to help."

"Of course." Farthing pulled out a handkerchief and cleaned his glasses. "It appears the boy's remained stable, so I'd say the splenectomy went fine. In time, he should recover fully. I'm afraid things are a bit more touch-and-go with the Patterson girl though. You might want to get another round of renal function tests."

Lance nodded. Some might find Farthing's fatherly oversight a bit intrusive, but Lance appreciated his attention to detail. His reviews were always offered in the spirit of helpfulness. "Thank you, John. I'll check on her condition after I talk to the spleen patient's family. Do you know where I can find them?"

"At the Family Resource Center." Farthing put on his glasses. "I'm headed that direction. I'll walk with you."

They strode briskly down the hall. "Things haven't gone so smoothly for the patients up at Sierra Memorial."

"I haven't heard. What's up?"

"An elderly gentleman with internal bleeding died earlier this morning."

"So, now it's two fatalities." Lance shook his head. "All things considered, it could have been worse."

"And still might. The other two patients there aren't much better off. Did you hear about the Jane Doe?" He worked to match pace with Lance's longer-legged gait.

"No." Lance scrolled through the patient chart while half-attending to the conversation.

"A young woman with no identification and apparently, no luggage. Not even a phone. Who doesn't carry a phone these days?"

"There are days I'd like to leave mine behind."

"I guess they're combing the crash site in hopes of finding something, but in the meantime … I can't even remember the last time we had a Jane Doe."

Lance looked up from the chart. "Technically, *we* don't. Sierra Memorial does."

They reached the elevator, and Farthing stopped to press the call button while Lance continued down the corridor. "She may become ours, if they get her stabilized enough to transfer."

Lance turned back with a surrendering shrug. "And when she wakes up, we can ask her what her name is." For the time being, it was out of their hands.

When he reached the Family Resource Center near the hospital's main hub, Lance found Pastor Mark Lindmeyer talking with the boy's parents and stepped up to join them. Lance liked Mark and attended his church whenever his Sunday schedule allowed. Over the next twenty minutes, the foursome reviewed lab tests and CT results. Lance was grateful he could assure the parents of their son's steady improvement and long-term prognosis.

When Lance excused himself, the pastor accompanied him down the polished corridor back toward ICU.

"It must have been pretty rough last night," Mark said.

"It was busy all right, but things went smoothly like you hope they will when something like this happens."

Mark nodded. "They showed the crash site on TV this morning. It's amazing the bus driver was the only casualty."

"Unfortunately, a second victim passed away this morning, and the hospital in Wakeville has two others that are still critical."

"We'll continue to pray then." Mark's eyebrows rose. "Do you know if they have a chaplain up there? Maybe I should make a trek up to Sierra Memorial."

That was so like Mark—jumping in to help wherever needed. Lance smiled, then remembered the Jane Doe. "One of the injured hasn't been identified yet. You can pray that situation gets resolved soon."

Mark's interest turned to concern. "Someone's unidentified? What happens then?"

"Oh, they'll figure it out. You know. Fingerprints, dental records. There are lots of ways to identify someone. But her family needs to be notified and every hour that goes by—"

A chirp on Lance's phone interrupted. A text from the Blood Bank in the east wing: Urgent need for O-Neg. Can you come in?

"I'll let you take care of that," Mark said, side-stepping toward the elevators. "You should come to home group tonight. It would give you a chance to relax a bit—decompress, as they say—and we could pray for you."

Lance clicked off the message. "Sure, I could probably do that."

"Let me know if there's anything else I can do."

"Thanks. I will." Lance picked up his pace on the way to the Blood Bank. Pastor Mark cared deeply, so he would never think of declining his prayers. All too often, though, his own seemed painfully inadequate, like those he'd cried out when Marla was near death. Mere Band-aids applied to a severed limb. In the years since her passing, his conversations with God had dwindled—something best left to the clergy, while he focused on his own skill set.

SEVEN

Dalton's charms were growing on me. Maybe it was the effect of inhaling its crisp mountain air or the serenity of my morning walk through its quiet streets. No harsh traffic. No pressures or deadlines. Such a contrast to the stressful uneasiness that had swelled in me during Brock's call. But I wouldn't blame that on Brock. He needed a respite too.

My spontaneous decision to make this trip wasn't just about reconnecting with Dad. There was a sense of urgency behind it too—I had to get away from there. Away from … something I couldn't quite put my finger on. Worst of all, trying to remember it was like trying to focus on a tiny pinprick of light—almost visible in my periphery, but vanishing when focused upon.

Dalton's serenity was a far more pleasant diversion. It had proven it deserved better than my initial designation of Nowhereville.

Maybe when Brock arrived tonight, he would also begin to benefit from Dalton's charms. He'd been under so much stress all season, becoming focused to the point of obsession about his chances at a pro-football career. Taking a week away from Hillman might do him a lot of good. Of course, Abbi's disappearance needed a quick resolution too, but I couldn't help feeling relieved that I was nowhere near the hub of the investigation.

A crisp breeze could be heard high in the pines that sheltered the north edge of Mrs. Wilton's property, but all other aspects of the place exuded peace, quiet and contentment. While I walked up the long cobbled drive approaching the old mansion, I enjoyed the sun's warmth on my face. Soon, I caught bits of piano music emanating from inside the house. I tuned my ears to the easy melody and climbed the steps to the front door. The tune was an old hymn I recognized from childhood, though the name escaped me. It seemed a shame to interrupt, so I paused on the porch and listened to the familiar chord progressions.

When the chorus concluded, I opened the door and stepped inside. The sliding doors of the room on the right were open to reveal a glossy black baby grand piano and a full-sized harp, both centered amid a lavish décor in soft rosy pink hues. An over-abundance of ivory lace curtains, swags, and doilies seemed to cover every surface.

Mrs. Wilton sat at the piano, fingers flying as she revived the chorus and swayed with each press of the foot pedals. The setting might have called for a Victorian gown, but she wore her simple house dress and bedroom slippers —the same attire I'd noticed at breakfast. The scene warmed me all the way through, even with my sore shoulder.

At the sound of the door closing, Mrs. Wilton glanced

up with a smile and adjusted her glasses. "You remember this song?"

"Kind of. It's a hymn, right?"

"It's *Softly and Tenderly*, one of my favorites. But then I have a lot of favorites." She pointed to a chair beside the doorway. "Have a seat, my dear."

I sat and rested the box of pie on my lap. Next to me, an antique pitcher and bowl sat atop a doily on a small end table. But my attention focused on the harp. "Do you play this also?"

"Oh yes, I've played the harp nearly as long as I can remember, but this—" She ran her fingers swiftly along the keys. "Well, playing this handsome instrument may have converted me."

Did she mean to imply that she hadn't played a piano before? I blinked, then chose to let the odd comment pass. "I'd love to hear the harp. Would you mind playing something on it?"

"Not at all. I was playing it earlier while you were out." She went to its upholstered stool and set aside a doily draped across the seat. Flexing her fingers, she made a long, slow strum across the strings creating a heavenly sound that resonated right through me.

The song began simply. It wasn't a tune I'd ever heard before. The harmony felt both poignant and uplifting. Quietly and gradually the music grew in complexity, with joyous swells of great emotion that flowed from the strings and filled the house. I marveled that such depth could flow from a single instrument. Like the current of a stream, it swept me along with delicate splashes of high notes and warm swirling currents in the lower range. So beautiful, and poetic in a way words could not describe.

Several enthralling minutes passed, and after a final sweeping lift of emotion, the strings slowly faded to silence.

"That … was … amazing." Tears brimmed my eyes. "I've never heard anything like it. Is it classical? Who wrote it?"

Mrs. Wilton's eyes crinkled as she smiled. "They were known as the Sons of Korah."

"I've never heard of them."

"Brave men." Her eyes raised as if drawing on a memory. "Loyal warriors of David's army, and as you see, also gifted song writers." She stood and replaced the doily. "Many people think David wrote all the Psalms, but a few like this one, were written by others. Nowadays, it's known as Psalm 46." She tapped a finger at her lower lip. "I don't recall the original title."

"Wait a minute." I rotated on the chair as she walked by. "Are you talking about King David from the Bible?"

"Yes, indeed." She paused at the door to the foyer and lifted her chin with a slight sniff. "You know, I think our soup is about ready. Are you hungry for some lunch?"

Mrs. Wilton's quirkiness had struck again. This time, I didn't let the matter go. "So you're saying King David's warriors wrote the music you just played? I thought we only knew the words of the Psalms. No one knows the music, do they?"

She smiled. "Oh, I wouldn't say 'no one.'" She ambled down the corridor to the kitchen. "The real tragedy is that nowadays, no one remembers what a good singing voice David had."

There, she did it again. Sweet as Mrs. Wilton was, my grandad would have said that her boat wasn't securely tied to the pier.

I followed her into the kitchen and put my pie in the refrigerator. Then I helped set the table while she dished up bowls of steaming chicken and vegetable soup with a dollop of sour cream on top.

"Stir it in to make the broth creamy," she said.

While savoring its richness, I remembered Brock's impending arrival. "Oh, I almost forgot. My boyfriend is on his way here today."

"Perhaps this is why you're feeling uneasy."

"No." My denial had a questioning lilt that made me sound unconvinced. "What I mean is, I feel fine. I'm glad he's coming. We've only been dating a few weeks, but I've grown to depend on him quite a lot. It'll be good to have him here."

"Well then, I'll make sure a room is ready."

"And we'll be leaving tomorrow."

"Yes, I know."

Why did she always say things like that? How did she know? But I didn't pursue my questions. I chose instead to let it go and focus on enjoying my lunch.

"Just one thing," she added a few minutes later. "Be sure to lock your door tonight. It's best to keep temptation at bay."

I stopped in the middle of lifting the spoon to my mouth. "Of course." Not that it was any of her business.

Besides, her advice seemed more motherly than invasive. It raised the beginnings of a smile to my mouth while she wasn't looking.

I passed the afternoon in my room, reading in preparation for a Microbiology class that would start with the new semester. Cheri texted the phone number of the investigators and I stared at it for a minute wondering what kind of help I could be to them. For all I knew, they might have already gathered enough information from others at the party. I had nothing more to offer. Nothing.

After a minute of conflicted indecision, I put the phone down and turned my attention back to the life-cycle of tardigrades.

The only other interruption was late in the afternoon when Brock texted. He was still a few hours away but wanted the address of the inn. Other than occasional sounds of Mrs. Wilton puttering in the house, the day passed quietly.

After supper, Mrs. Wilton asked if I wanted to sit in the parlor with her while I ate my pie. I sat on the sofa while she chose one of the wing chairs, switched on the table lamp, and slid a bag out from beside it. In a moment, she'd retrieved a ball of thread and crochet hook which held the start of something lacy.

"What are you making?" I asked. It looked a lot like a doily.

"At first, I thought another table runner would be nice." She extended a length of ivory string from the ball. "But now I think a nice little doily might be best." She adjusted her glasses. "If I change my mind again, it won't matter much, since my table runners are basically long, narrow doilies." She smiled with a wink. "You crochet?"

"No, I don't have time for things like that in college and probably wouldn't have the patience anyway."

"Patience does seem to be in short supply these days." She worked the hook, her slender fingers moving with deft precision.

"And then there's all those tiny little stitches," I added. "I'd be so stressed about making a mistake and having to unravel everything to try to make it right."

"Mmm, yes. Mistakes do happen from time to time." The elder woman's brow pinched as she held her work out at arm's length. "It's definitely easier if you catch them right away."

"So, what do you do if you've gone too far along and cannot go back?"

"Cannot?" Mrs. Wilton turned her gaze to me. "Life offers people so many choices. It's unfortunate that some folks put undue focus on their mistakes, believing they cannot be made right again. Sometimes, all it takes is seeing the options they still have."

The conversation seemed to have shifted. Were we still talking about crochet? I studied the wedge of coconut custard on the tip of my fork.

Apparently unaware, Mrs. Wilton resumed brightly, "At any rate, I'm glad you decided to stay for another night. I was hoping we'd get another chance to talk."

"Oh?"

"There's a scripture that the Lord has been pressing on

my heart ever since you arrived. I wonder if you've heard it before."

Here we go. I paused, resting the fork on my plate.

"I can't think of where the verse is exactly, but Jesus says, 'There is nothing hidden which will not be revealed, nor has anything been kept secret but that it should come to light.'"

"Sorry, I wouldn't know where to find that verse either."

She stopped her work to chuckle. "Oh, that doesn't matter. It's enough for me to know Jesus said it." She refocused on her thread and hook. "I'm quite sure He brought it to mind because He means something about you is hidden—or has been hidden from you."

"I can't imagine what that would be." Even as I spoke, the missing girl from the New Year's party came to mind. Was it possible Mrs. Wilton could key in on something significant for the police investigation?

"Not to worry," Mrs. Wilton's voice soothed. "I'm sure it will become clear when it needs to."

Was God trying to reassure that Abbi would be found? And if so, would she be dead or alive? In my experience, God's assurances didn't always mean good outcomes. But what if Mrs. Wilton had a certain kind of clairvoyance? Did it matter that she liked to attribute her gift to the Divine? The world was full of strange, unexplainable things.

I cut another segment of coconut cream pie with my fork. "It's weird you should talk about this, because my roommate called earlier with news that a girl from school is missing. Do you think maybe God plans to reveal where she is?"

Mrs. Wilton's brow pinched as she considered this. Finally, she resumed her crocheting. "The Lord knows about the missing girl, there's no doubt about that. But I'm quite sure He's giving this message to you, Penny." She cast another glance my direction.

Her words gave me a chill. "I'm not hiding anything."

"I think rather that something has been hidden from you."

I attempted to swallow a gradual swell of frustration. "Well, if God or Jesus or whoever is going to reveal it, why doesn't He? Why is He keeping it a secret?"

"I don't know, child. His ways are not our ways."

Hmmff. I had to agree with her last statement, though. God's ways certainly didn't correspond with mine. I didn't respond and soon Mrs. Wilton attended to her lace again.

I placed my fork back on the plate. That's when we heard a knock at the door.

Brock had arrived.

EIGHT

Setting the pie plate on the coffee table, I went to the door, intending to give Brock a warm welcome with arms around his neck. When I opened it, though, he pushed in with a duffle bag, his handsome face clouded like a thunderstorm about to descend.

I stepped back and tried to give him a smile. "I'm so glad you made it okay."

"It took forever to find this place," he muttered. "There's no sign, and the only streetlight is halfway down the block."

"It's a small town."

He pulled his cap off, loosening dark waves of hair that fell over his furrowed brow. "You could have given better directions."

"Sorry." I reached to take his bag, but he set it beside the door.

Mrs. Wilton appeared at my side. "Hello. Welcome to Wayfarer's Inn, Mister—?"

"Harper," Brock and I responded in unison. I chuckled and Brock's disposition lightened a smidge. At least he managed a brief smile for Mrs. Wilton's benefit.

"May I help with your coat, Mr. Harper?"

"Sure." He removed it and loaded her arm, nearly engulfing her tiny frame. Then he topped it with his scarf.

She waddled to the closet under the stairs.

Brock wiped his boots on the rug and whispered while she was out of earshot. "We need to talk."

I took hold of his arm. "Later. You just got here."

His mouth twisted, but he held his tongue.

When Mrs. Wilton emerged from the closet, I resumed a normal tone. "Mrs. Wilton and I were visiting in the parlor. Would you like to join us?"

I took Brock's arm and steered him to the sofa, hoping he would turn on the charm I knew him to be capable of. He sat next to me, and Mrs. Wilton returned to her chair and picked up her crocheting.

"I trust you had a pleasant journey, Mr. Harper?" She squinted through her glasses to adjust the thread on her hook.

"You can call me Brock." He glanced around the room with a critical eye. "It was fine, thanks."

Mrs. Wilton didn't seem to notice his scrutiny of her home. "I understand you are a student at the same college Penny attends."

"Yeah. Hillman Oaks," he replied. "Just outside Phoenix."

"We met after a football game the weekend before Thanksgiving," I added. Brock's posture seemed awkward, like he was unable to relax. I patted his knee, attempting to settle the agitation I assumed came from hours of driving. "I went to the game because my roommate's cousin plays on the team. Cheri—that's my roommate—she introduced us." I glanced toward Brock. "That was an exciting evening, wasn't it?"

He nodded, but his thoughts seemed to be elsewhere.

"It was the night the Panthers made it into the division championships. When we started seeing each other I had to take a crash course in football. Especially after their big win." I draped my arm on Brock's shoulder and smoothed the hair on the back of his head. He didn't notice. "Just last week they played in the Oasis Bowl. The press coverage has been so exciting. Life around this guy has become a whirlwind." I pulled my arm back and picked up the pie from the coffee table. "Yup. It all started with that game before Thanksgiving."

Mrs. Wilton glanced up from her handiwork. "So, you hadn't known each other from class studies?"

"No, but we did discover we were attending the same humanities class without knowing it." I glanced to Brock and elbowed his ribs. "It's a popular course—lots of students."

Why was Brock so distracted? I offered him a forkful of coconut cream. "Want a bite?"

He waved it off.

Mrs. Wilton paused her work. "I'm not familiar with that. What is a humanities class?"

"It's a combination of related subjects that includes studies on culture, the arts, language, philosophy—"

Brock suddenly popped up off the sofa. "Excuse me, but I need to talk with Penny—in private—so I hope it's okay if we head up to our room now." He grasped my hand and pulled me to stand so fast, I barely managed to set my plate back on the table.

"You mean, your rooms," Mrs. Wilton said, peering over her glasses.

"Of course, Mrs. Wilton," I assured her. "Sorry to cut our chat short. Brock is tired from the long drive. Thank you for everything."

He pulled me away from the sofa, his hand grasping mine with intense heat. Perhaps he was coming down with something.

Mrs. Wilton's eyes seemed to be framed in question marks.

"See you in the morning, then?" I said in a vain attempt to normalize the scene.

She studied us as he led me out to the hall and grabbed his duffle bag. We went upstairs and into my room where he closed the door and finally released his grip of my hand.

"You really didn't need to be so rude." I rubbed my over-squeezed palm.

"I didn't come here to give lessons on college courses to some old lady." His voice was low and even.

I walked to the far side of the bed and began to lower the blinds. "Why *did* you come?"

"To help you patch things up with your dad, remember?"

"I didn't know I needed help with that." My tone had a snide edge, and I knew it. Brock's silence meant he was glaring, so I kept my face to the window and softened my tone. "So, what did you need to talk to me about?"

He didn't answer right away, but I heard him pace back and forth behind me. "We have to talk about the New Year's Eve party—and about us."

"What's to talk about?" I spun toward him, and the expression on his face made my stomach unsettled. As if he were about to reveal Mrs. Wilton's "hidden things."

"I think you had a little too much to drink that night. We all did. Since you don't normally drink, I thought you might be feeling bad about what happened."

What was he talking about? I had one drink. One. In fact, I didn't even finish it. Tyler's girlfriend mistook my drink for hers and downed the last third or so. Now that he'd brought it up, I remembered that part clearly.

But other things were not so clear. In fact, much of that evening remained very foggy.

"First of all, I wasn't drunk." I stated it firmly, looking him in the eye, but his hard expression did not change. "And I don't know what you're talking about." Even as I spoke, I remembered Cheri telling me that Tyler's girlfriend had disappeared. "Wait. Are you talking about that girl, Abbi? Cheri told me she's missing, but—" Suddenly my palms were sweaty. "She probably went somewhere for semester break. She'll turn up, right?" I rubbed my hands on my sleeves. The room had become overly warm—stuffy.

Brock seemed to be studying me, his expression grim. "Are you sure you don't remember?"

"The party? Of course I do. Some of it, anyway. Why are you making a big deal out of it?"

"It only became a big deal when you left campus

without a word. I figured you were angry or … embarrassed … or something. I thought we were in this together, but if you don't want to talk about it…" He looked away and stuffed his hands in his pockets.

So he was offended? It seemed he expected either an apology or confession, neither of which seemed appropriate for this situation. "What is it you want me to say?"

He turned back to me. "Can't you just be glad I'm here?"

"I was. I am. You drove all day to be here, and I appreciate that."

"I drove all the way here because you mean a lot to me, Penny."

"I know that."

"You had me worried when you left town without a word."

"Sorry. I didn't mean to worry you."

He came around the end of the bed and put his hands on my shoulders. "Okay then. We don't need to talk about it anymore tonight." His voice softened. "Besides, more than anything else, I was looking forward to spending some quality time with you." He pulled me close. "I miss you when you're not with me."

I surrendered to his embrace, burying my face in his shoulder. "I miss you too, and I'd rather not spend our time arguing."

"You're right. We'll start fresh tomorrow."

"That would be nice." I pulled back to study his eyes.

He stroked my hair, and smiled with the same

adoration that had first melted my heart toward him. "You know, we've never had a chance to be together alone like this." He glanced about the room. "It's not exactly the Taj Mahal, but what do you think?" He tipped my chin up with his hand and kissed me gently.

I thought about telling him the Taj Mahal was a tomb, but it would only irritate him. Besides, I knew what he meant, and even though he thought sex shouldn't be a big deal, it was. I wasn't ready to take our relationship to that level.

I looked up at his handsome face, his eyes like deep pools of expectancy. "You know I'm not ready for that."

"Why not?"

At the moment, with his hands caressing my neck and face, I struggled to focus on the reason. "I've already told you before. It's too soon. We're still getting to know each other, and besides, I … I promised Mrs. Wilton I would lock my door tonight."

His expression changed and he pulled back. "You what?"

The spell was broken. I took hold of his arm and turned him around. "Goodnight, Brock. It's for the best, you know."

"Really?"

"Really."

At the door, he protested, but I hushed him with an index finger to my lips. "Quiet now. Mrs. Wilton is right downstairs, remember?"

I handed his bag over and closed the door, listening

until I heard him close his own, then I turned the lock. No point in tempting fate.

I took a deep breath and paced the room, trying to figure out why Brock thought I would become angry or embarrassed about the New Year's Eve Party. It wasn't a memorable event. Why feel either of those things?

But I *had* caused a problem, one Brock had already mentioned. It seemed small from my point of view, but clearly it was significant to him. In spite of having told Cheri my travel plans, I'd left Brock out of the loop, and he had worried about me. Perhaps he felt added stress because of what happened to Abbi. At any rate, I hoped that tomorrow her disappearance would be explained, and everything would return to normal.

Just one thing, though. Brock hadn't been the one to mention Abbi's disappearance. I brought it up. When he started talking nonsense about me being drunk, it threw me off track initially, but shouldn't he have brought up the subject before I did?

I shook my head and tried to dismiss the feelings that didn't seem to match with facts. There was no point in making a big issue out of this.

Later, I washed up in the bathroom down the hall. When I came out, Brock stood, leaning against the wall, wearing a plain white t-shirt and long flannel pajama bottoms. His dark eyes were brooding again.

I crossed my arms. "You forget something?" It was difficult to warm up to him when he made me feel like I'd done something wrong.

"I can't help wondering if I made a mistake coming all the way out here."

Now what was he hinting at? "I don't know. You tell me." Another comment with a snide edge, but I was tired of his hot-and-cold treatment.

He glanced down and drug a toe across the carpet, apparently annoyed. "You've been challenging me ever since I arrived."

"I'm challenging you?" Maybe I was, but he had been the one to push first.

"Yeah, like you're doing right now." He straightened to stand in the narrow hall, leaving little room to pass by.

The subtle escalation had reached an uncomfortable level. Better to back down and let things cool. "I don't want to challenge you."

"Then what's the problem, Penny?" He tilted his head.

I avoided looking him in the eye. "I thought you said we were going to start fresh."

"Tomorrow. We'll start fresh tomorrow, but I have a feeling something's still bugging you."

"Okay, how about this? Why didn't you tell me about Tyler's girlfriend going missing?" I blurted it out and immediately felt another flash of déjà vu. I'd had this confrontation with him before. It had played out just like this. But when? We'd never been standing in this hallway before.

A moment of surprise crossed his face, exactly as I knew it would. "I didn't know you'd heard about it." His arms dropped and he loosened his stance, glancing about as if searching for words. "I planned to tell you, but I didn't want you to be worried."

"Worried?" The déjà vu was fading.

Brock's eyes darted to every corner. "You know. Worried that there's some crazed killer on the loose."

"You mean, she's dead?"

"No, no. I didn't mean that." Flustered at first, he recovered quickly. "She's missing, that's all … but they'll find her. I'm sure they'll find her soon." He reached toward me, as if to offer comfort, but I stayed at the bathroom door.

He seemed uneasy. I didn't know what to make of it. "Let's talk about it tomorrow, Brock."

He let his hands drop and didn't say anything more as I maneuvered past him and down the hall to my room.

NINE

Lance walked up the hall from the elevators and spotted the officer waiting for him in the alcove next to the ICU desk. Even dressed in plainclothes, his official status was evident. Jill had called about his arrival while Lance finished up at the blood bank, but she had no other information. Undoubtedly, it had something to do with the investigation into the bus crash.

The officer's serious expression suggested something new may have gone wrong. It was bad enough two people had already died and two others were hanging on by a thread. What now?

As he approached, the man stood and extended his hand. "You're Dr. Lance Doyle?" He had a gray moustache and salt-and-pepper hair in need of a trim.

"I am. I understand you're looking for me?" Lance shook his hand.

The officer reached in his coat pocket and pulled out a badge. "I'm Sergeant Clemens, an investigator with the Sheriff's Department. I've been asked to do some follow-up on behalf of investigators at the Maricopa County Sheriff's Department in Arizona."

Lance flinched. Penny was in Arizona.

The investigator referred to his clipboard as he continued. "They're looking into the disappearance of a young woman—"

"Penny?" Lance was way ahead of him. "What's happened?"

Sergeant Clemens looked up from his notes. "We need to speak to your daughter, sir. Her roommate told the Maricopa County officers she's here with you, and we have reason to believe she's among the last people to see the missing woman."

"Here?" Lance tried to shift gears with what he heard. "Penny's not here. You said her roommate—?" His mind fumbled. Who did this guy say was missing?

The sergeant jotted something on the clipboard. "Have you heard from your daughter recently?"

"Wait … is Penny missing?" He grabbed the officer's arm.

Clemens' countenance softened. "Doctor, I don't have any information to suggest *your* daughter's missing. If you haven't seen her yet, perhaps she'll show up later today. The information was provided by..." He referenced his notes. "… a Cheri Gilman. Do you know her?"

Realizing he still gripped the officer's arm, Lance let go and stepped back. "No, not really. My daughter rarely contacts me. If her roommate thinks she's here, then where is she?"

"We'll get it figured out, sir. Like I said, she may be on her way." Clemens pulled a card from his pocket. "If you do hear from your daughter, would you please give us a call right away? We're helping follow up on the Arizona case and have some questions for her."

"Of course."

The officer left and Lance stared at the card for a moment, his mind trying to catch up with what he'd heard. Where was Penny? He should call her. Of course, others had probably tried that already. Like the roommate. What did the man say her name was? Sharon? Shelly? Neither seemed right.

He rubbed his forehead in frustration, then pulled out his phone and punched Penny's name. The call went straight to voice mail.

"Hi!" Her recording was bright and cheerful. So unlike the monotone she used around him. "I'm not answering right now, but maybe I'll call you later, if you leave a nice message." Then she laughed just before the message tone cut in.

He hung up, planning to try again later. In the meantime, he'd have to figure out what to say when he got through to her.

The rest of the afternoon dragged by, as Lance tried to focus on his patients. He pulled into his driveway just before six o'clock, weary from fretful hours wondering where Penny could be. He'd tried calling her four times and left a text as well. Why didn't she answer?

Hopes that she might already be at home faded as he pulled his car into the garage. Entering the kitchen, he flipped on the light and dropped his keys on the counter. As always, the house was dark and quiet, his daily reminder of the void that had followed Marla's passing.

But today was worse. Today, Penny was supposed to be back home.

Their separation had been his fault. He had been out of his element trying to help her untangle the grief and anger that simmered behind her eyes. She'd pulled away like a hot air balloon straining at its tethers, resisting his every effort to hold her close. One by one, she had snipped the constraints until she could fly away, and feeling powerless, he had let her go.

If only Marla were here.

He opened the refrigerator, but he wasn't hungry. What he really needed was … what? His brain wouldn't focus. Then he remembered Pastor Mark's invitation to the home fellowship meeting.

He felt torn between the prayer he needed and waiting by the front window, in case Penny arrived. Closing the refrigerator, his eyes landed on the grocery list stuck on the door.

There was an idea. If she overlooked his text message, at least he could put a note on the front door. He tore off a sheet from the notepad and wrote: Penny, I heard you might be on your way home. I'm nearby, so let yourself in, and give me a call. I've missed you. Love, Dad.

He taped it to the front door glass, then grabbed his keys and went out to the car. As the overhead door opened, he noticed someone sitting in an SUV in front of a neighbor's house across the street. A shadowy figure in the driver's seat looked his way. An investigator watching the house, perhaps? He tried to act natural as he got in his car. Had the vehicle been there when he arrived, or had this guy followed him home? He had no idea.

Lance backed out of the garage, then punched the remote to close the door. The person, a male, slouched against his seat and pulled a ball cap low over his face. Avoidance?

Lance made a mental note of the license, but didn't know what else he should do. As he drove away, the SUV stayed put.

When he pulled up to Mark and Jackie's home, there were no other cars. Was the meeting somewhere else? Or maybe he was too early? He glanced at his watch, suddenly uncertain of the scheduled meeting time. Should he knock on their door? They might be trying to finish supper, or get things set up for the meeting.

He decided to wait a few minutes in case someone else showed up. He slouched a bit, and leaned back against the head rest, staring at the roof liner. Maybe the guy in the SUV had been doing the same thing. Killing time waiting in his car.

Lance shook his head. This situation with the investigators had put him on edge. He considered trying to call Penny again, but would it do any good? Her phone was off, or the battery dead. Or maybe … maybe she didn't want to talk to him.

And why did her roommate tell the investigators she was here? Was she on her way, like the officer suggested? Did she really want to come home again?

A tap at the passenger window grabbed Lance's attention. It was Mark. "Hey, glad you made it."

Lance got out of the car. "Sorry if I'm too early."

"Nonsense. Come on in. I was just bringing out the trash." Mark led the way up the driveway. "I'm glad I noticed you sitting there. How did today go?"

"Not what I expected."

"Your patients not doing so well?"

"No, they're fine. It's actually about Penny."

"Penny?" Mark opened the front door and held it for him. "You've heard from her?"

Jackie was arranging a tray of refreshments on the coffee table in the living room as they entered. Lance told them about the visit from the officer and his attempts to reach Penny that day. He even told them about the person parked in front of the neighbor's house, and how it unnerved him.

Mark placed a hand on Lance's shoulder. "If you want, we could drive back and see if the guy's still there."

Lance shook his head. "There's no need to interrupt the meeting. It might be nothing more than my imagination getting the better of me. I only wish I knew where Penny was right now."

Mark and Jackie offered their comfort, and as people arrived for the evening's meeting, he became enveloped in the warmth of their fellowship. He gathered strength from their encouragement to press on for answers that seemed elusive. Throughout the evening, as the group sang and prayed for each other, his cares were lifted. Together with the group, he found new hope and encouragement through their tears, hugs and uplifting words from the Scripture.

When the meeting closed, Lance went home feeling full and ready for the day to come. The SUV was gone when he approached the house. Like a specter of his fears, it seemed to have vanished as a result of the group's prayers.

But the house stood dark and silent. No sign Penny had been by. He pulled into the garage and got out. Stepping back to the open overhead door, he lifted his face to the night sky. "Where are you, Penny? Are you really coming home?"

Only God knew, and for the moment, that would have to be enough.

TEN

B reakfast with Brock and Mrs. Wilton was quite nice —well, almost. Brock made a fuss about his bacon being overdone and rolled his eyes over the fact that the pancake syrup wasn't pure maple. Then he pointed out a stain on the centerpiece doily while Mrs. Wilton was out of the room. "Good thing we're heading out this morning."

"Just let it go, Brock. This place is fine."

"For you, maybe, but I'm this close to signing a pro contract, babe." He measured an inch with his fingers. "And that means a future spent with all the right people in all the right places." He waved a hand about the room. "This hole-in-the-wall is for losers."

"I thought we were starting fresh today."

He gave me an abrupt stare but kept any further discontent to himself.

After breakfast, Brock went upstairs while I helped Mrs. Wilton clear the dining table and tidy the kitchen. "I've really enjoyed my stay here, Mrs. Wilton." I hung the tea towel to dry. "I don't suppose I'll be back this way again, but I'll remember your hospitality always."

Mrs. Wilton smiled and put her hand on my arm.

"That's very sweet, but there's something more important for you to remember, my dear."

"Oh?" I reacted to her more serious tone. "What's that?"

"God loves you, Penny. He knows everything, and He loves you."

I tried to smile, but drew back when unexpected tears threatened to brim. Sentiments like hers were familiar. A repeated litany I'd heard all my life—but they rang hollow when things happened that showed how little God actually paid attention.

She released my arm and her smile softened with compassion. "When the time is right, and God reveals the things that have been hidden, you will know how much He loves both you and your father." With that, she went back to the sink, softly humming a tune. In spite of her quirkiness, she was a kind woman—someone I hoped God would take time to care about.

I wiped my eyes and started toward the door.

"Oh." Mrs. Wilton turned, raising a soapy wet hand from the dishwater. "And don't be too surprised if we see each other again. You never know."

"That's right. You never know." It was a sweet notion that lifted my spirits.

Later, while we loaded Brock's car, I paused to study the sky from the bottom of the porch steps. In only a moment, I detected the soft press of a cat stroking his back against my leg. "Kitty. Where have you been?"

He looked up, blinking his radiant blue eyes, and I crouched to pet him. "Good Kitty."

Brock came down the steps with my suitcase. "We're not taking a cat along."

I chuckled at his good-natured rib. "Are you sure?"

"Absolutely." He maneuvered past us. "I'm allergic, remember?"

I stroked Kitty's head one last time. "Sorry, but I have to go now. Take care of Mrs. Wilton, okay?"

I stood and Kitty smoothed against my leg once more before heading into the tangle of shrubs beside the walkway.

It marked a poignant close to the end of my time in Dalton.

So much for *Nowhereville*.

Soon we were on the road to Barrett, heading up a mountain pass and over to the next valley. Overcast skies draped the highest peaks in white. It began to snow softly along the winding way, but it felt good to be back in my home state. Colorado's byways always held new wonders at every bend. Rounding a curve would bring mesmerizing glimpses of snowy peaks into view. A moment later, those would be cut off by sheer cliff faces that hugged the roadside. We even stopped once for a photo at the unexpected sight of mountain sheep standing among fallen boulders in a side canyon.

For a long time we chatted easily about the trip, the weather, the view—everything but the topic I knew we needed to broach.

Eventually the conversation lulled.

Brock spoke first. "I want you to know I planned to tell you about Abbi's disappearance yesterday." He shifted to a lower gear and kept his eyes on the road. "I just forgot about it when I arrived last night."

"I suppose Tyler must be pretty upset."

"The investigators have been a real pain. They had us both down at the station for hours, and while we were there, they snooped around his house."

"Really?" I turned to study his profile. "What were they looking for?"

"I don't know." He swallowed. "Evidence from … the fight, I guess."

I gasped. "They had a fight?"

Brock kept his eyes straight ahead, working his jaw. "C'mon, Penny. *They* didn't fight. You did."

"What?" My breath caught in my throat.

"Don't worry. The investigators didn't find anything."

"Brock, I did *not* fight with her! I don't even know her. Why would we fight?"

"You don't remember because of the booze."

"I already told you I wasn't drunk. Why don't you believe me?" My voice rose, like the heat that suddenly climbed my neck.

"I was there. Tyler and I both saw what happened." He sounded condescending now. "Besides, we already told the investigators all about that night."

Panic gripped me, choking off my ability to reply. No wonder Cheri said the investigators wanted to talk to me. They might even want to arrest me, and my fragmented memory provided no conclusive defense. They could easily take Brock's word over mine.

"Don't worry. I'm not going to turn you in." He reached over and put his hand on my shoulder.

"What?" I jerked away to lean against the car door. "Turn me in? I had nothing to do with Abbi's disappearance!"

Why was he saying such things? I pinched my eyes to shut off the sudden flow of tears and choked as they caught in my throat instead.

What if I didn't know myself? What if…? My memory might be fractured, but I shook my head against any suggestion of doubt.

"Fine then." Brock's voice cut through my thoughts. "So much for trying to be helpful."

He glared at the road while I stared at a dry creek bed out my side window. Rocks and weeds blurred as we passed by.

I tried to recapture my memories of that evening. Was there any time when Abbi had been angry at anyone? Could *she* have started the fight? She seemed to be in full party mode, laughing, making numerous toasts and hanging on Tyler as if she were a necktie. She'd even come in a costume, though it wasn't that type of party. Some kind of glittery, flapper-style dress with a headband to match. If it wasn't a costume, it certainly suited her flamboyance.

Abbi did everything possible to remain the center of attention that night, and it seemed to work on everyone, including Brock. I recalled having some embarrassment at the girl's obvious behavior, but mostly I ignored her.

Late in the evening, after she finished my one-and-only

drink, I found her asleep in a chair, one leg draped over the arm and the slit of her dress exposing a bit more thigh than it should. I laid a napkin across her lap thinking that, for all the hoopla, she couldn't even manage to stay awake until midnight.

But then what happened? I closed my eyes and reached for the memory, but the only sensations my mind conjured were more like some kind of dream. Shifting shadows. Shouting. A jerk of my shoulder. Dizziness and swirling that threatened to turn my stomach…

I jolted upright and opened my eyes to the road. In my periphery, Brock glanced my way with a concerned expression though he said nothing.

Were these disjointed bits and pieces actually snatches of memory about the fight, or were they some kind of fiction my mind had created? It was true my shoulder ached yesterday, but had it bothered me the day before? And what about the bruise on my hip? What if Brock was right? Was it possible to have a physical altercation with someone and not remember it?

No. I wasn't the fighting type, and I refused the notion that a partial drink would impair me so much. Besides, even if I had gotten agitated enough to take it to that level, it wouldn't explain Abbi's disappearance. Something else had happened. Surely, even the police would realize that.

Brock kept glancing toward me, his hands clenching the steering wheel as if to reshape it. Ever since he arrived last night, he'd been difficult, even testy. Where was the fun, enthusiastic football player I had met just weeks ago? The guy who thought we were destined for each other, like

Cleopatra and Antony? Was all this tension due to pressures from their winning season? He was certainly a guy used to getting his way, and I'd been around him long enough to see the tactics he used on others. The same ones he bragged about using on the field. Press. Maneuver. Control.

Was he now using them on me?

A sharp lump formed in my throat—one too painful to swallow.

ELEVEN

My mind wandered in sullen silence until Brock pulled off the highway into the rustic mountain town of Barrett. My eyes skimmed the rooftops of bungalows, cabins, and small Victorians lining Main Street while my thoughts focused on a different house on the other side of the next pass. Home.

Dad was there, keeping everything exactly as Mom would have, while living a life unaffected by how far we'd drifted apart. Initially, we had clung to each other, desperate to find meaning in our shared tragedy. But Dad found consolation by declaring faith in God's sovereign power, while I became convinced of His weakness and apathy. Over time, the swelling current of my disappointment in God had carried me to a distant shore.

Would Dad accept me while I held on to my reluctance of faith? Soon I'd have the answer. At the moment, as the remaining miles between us dwindled, home felt as far away as ever.

Brock tapped the plastic that covered the car's dashboard clock. "Hey, look at that. It's nearly noon."

He glanced my way, but I ignored him. As far as I was

concerned, his accusations about drunkenness and fighting with Tyler's girlfriend had earned an extended cold shoulder treatment.

"Are you hungry?" He held fast to his nonchalant act. "We could get some lunch before we head over the next pass."

I shifted from silence to apathy. "I don't care. Whatever you want."

"There may not be many options here. Good thing we're not fussy eaters." He smiled, perhaps pleased at having cracked my resolve.

"Whatever."

Downtown Barrett amounted to three blocks of vintage storefronts, with additional businesses and offices scattered on side streets. As Brock circled the downtown area to find parking, we discovered the bus station one street over from the main avenue. It was housed in an old windowed storefront wedged between a hardware store and barber shop.

He nodded toward it. "Good thing you don't have to wait in there all day."

I didn't argue, but given my current frame of mind, it would have been easier than he thought.

He parked opposite the station, in front of an abandoned lot between two weathered Victorians. My purse had tumbled back from the center console during our drive, so I pulled it out from behind the car seat.

"Why bother with your bag? You don't need it." Brock sounded impatient.

I looped the strap over my shoulder. "There's a gift

shop next to the café. I thought maybe I could get a little something for Dad. A Christmas gift." *Or peace offering.*

He tilted his head. "We don't have all day."

"One little shop won't take much time."

He resigned and, as we walked back toward Main Street, he reached for my hand, giving it an affectionate squeeze. I had always thrilled at the times his hand clasped mine, but today I recognized the charade. A play toward some unknown audience. Though I didn't resist the gesture, I didn't reciprocate either.

The café exuded a rustic European charm. Against one wall, a fragrant bakery display sat next to the register and filled the room with luscious aromas. From overhead, Parisian accordion music interspersed with the hubbub of lunch patrons.

The waitress, a girl about my age sporting spikey neon-yellow hair with black roots, led us to a small table at a narrow spot in the back of the room. Brock slumped into the chair on the side with the most room while I squeezed into the tight space opposite.

When the waitress returned a few minutes later, he ordered for us both. I wasn't hungry, but withheld a protest. Let him play the scene his way.

Brock stared around the room while drumming his fingers on the table. In Arizona, he would occasionally be approached for an autograph, especially since the championship win. Was he annoyed at his anonymity in Colorado? His phone chimed an incoming text, and he read it while the waitress delivered our drinks.

I thanked her and took a sip. "Who's it from?"

"Tyler." He tucked the phone back into his coat.

"Any news on Abbi?"

He twirled the straw in his glass. "Nah." His tone suggested he didn't expect new developments.

"What's Tyler's theory on why she disappeared?"

"That she probably decided to leave town without telling anyone—like you did." Another jab indicating he wasn't over it.

"But I told Cheri."

He poked at the ice with his straw. "But you didn't tell *me*."

"I didn't know it was that important. Are you still mad at me?"

"I'm pretty sure it's the other way around." His eyes were steady, challenging me.

"Brock, you've as much as accused me of being responsible for Abbi's disappearance." My voice rose. "How should I feel?"

"Not now," he warned through gritted teeth. "Let's eat our lunch and get out of here."

Whatever. I put my hands in my lap and stared at the coffee rings staining the table top.

He excused himself to find the restroom, and I noticed him reach into his coat on the way out. He was probably planning to call Tyler back, so why act secretive? Was he going to tell Tyler about accusing me? From the sound of it, Tyler already thought I was responsible too. And if they believed I was to blame, how many others did as well?

With elbows on the table, I held my head and forced myself not to groan.

Press, maneuver, control. Brock's football tactics had turned out to be his life tactics. I felt squeezed in a vise. How did I ever get mixed up with this guy?

It suddenly occurred to me I didn't need to be involved with him. Not any longer. The bus station was here—right around the corner.

I unwrapped the silverware and asked a passing waitress for a pen. In a hasty scribble, I wrote on the napkin. *This isn't going to work. Thanks for bringing me this far. I want to go home alone. It's for the best. Penny.*

Our sandwiches arrived as I finished the note, so I laid the napkin over his plate, and asked the waitress if they had a back door. The last thing I needed was to encounter Brock as I left.

"Is something wrong?" Her brown eyes widened.

"Not the food. It's just time he and I parted ways."

She offered a sympathetic nod and led me through the kitchen to a back door.

I exited onto a small wood platform two steps above the alley pavement. Pausing, I lifted my face to the sky and breathed in the crisp mountain air. *What do I do now?* It wasn't exactly a prayer, but I needed to get centered and calm the quivers in my gut.

I rested a hand on the rough railing, crusted with peeling paint. The texture seemed to trigger something inside my brain. As if a dam had suddenly burst, my heart began to pound. Dizziness threatened my footing. I gripped the rail and pinched my eyes shut against a swirling sensation that engulfed me. My equilibrium seemed to tilt. What was happening?

Then a strong hand gripped my shoulder from behind. With a harsh jerk, it spun me around, and I opened my eyes.

Brock held me in his grip, his face hostile, twisted with angry determination. His dark eyes pierced through me like poisoned darts.

Terror shot through my veins and my vision tunneled, closing off the alley and the sky. Instead, we were in a place that smelled vaguely like a workshop or toolshed.

I felt powerless to move under Brock's gaze. Judging by the look in his eyes and the snarl of his lip, my once-adoring boyfriend had become angry enough to kill me.

I drew a deep breath. One last chance to scream. The icy outdoor air hit my lungs and Brock dissolved before my eyes. I found myself standing in the alley once again, under a white winter sky.

I swallowed, hoping to calm my racing pulse, but the memory of Brock's threatening gaze didn't dissolve with the vision. I had actually seen that glare on his face. It was a memory of something real that happened between us, but where? And when? It wasn't my imagination. For some reason, I had forgotten this event—until now. His anger had been real, and I could still feel the pinch of his wrenching grip.

Stumbling in haste down the wooden platform, I stared in the direction of the nearest side street. *Get ahold of yourself. Think.* What would Brock do when he saw my note? Chase me down and drag me back to the car? Would I see that glare again?

I ran to the side street and turned toward the end of the

block, then realized the bus station would be the first place Brock would look.

Yes. He would look for me.

At the very least, he would be upset that I'd left him, the hero football player, publicly scorned. He would expect an apology, and I'd have to deal with his indignation on top of the gut-wrenching accusation he'd made.

Would he even drive me to my dad's house after this? He might choose instead to call the cops and tell them I was wanted in connection with Abbi's disappearance.

No, he wouldn't do that.

Or would he?

I dashed down the sidewalk and ducked into the nearest storefront. "New to You" was painted on the door. Any other day, a consignment shop would have been a fun diversion from the mundane.

Today was anything but mundane.

"Hello," called a cheery middle-aged woman from her place behind the counter. "May I help you find something?"

"Just looking." I maneuvered through some clothing racks, then realized none would hide me from view if Brock peered in the front windows. I headed to a row of tall shelves farther back and pretended to examine some vintage china while my mind raced. The bus wouldn't be here until late tonight. Would Brock search for me that long? Probably not, but where could I find a place to wait him out?

I picked up a teacup, pretending to shop, but my fingers trembled so I set it back down and moved to another shelf. Would my old bus ticket still be valid? I might have to purchase a new one. I reached into my bag for the slim case that held my credit ca—

Oh no!

I groped at the side pocket. *No, no, no!* My skin went cold at the realization that my bank cards and phone must have slipped out of the bag when it fell from the center console.

They were still in Brock's car.

TWELVE

T he clinic had been busy all morning with post-surgery follow-ups and new patients to be placed on Lance's surgical schedule. As he exited from a consult with his associate, Dr. Baird, he clicked the next appointment on his tablet's roster.

"Dr. Doyle," a familiar voice called from behind.

He turned to see Sergeant Clemens approaching.

"Sergeant. Good to see you again." Lance studied the older man's expression. *Especially if you're bringing good news.*

"Can you spare a moment? I have some new information." The sergeant tapped a stack of papers on his clipboard.

"Of course."

Clemens glanced at the surrounding bustle of activity. "Perhaps in your office?"

"It's right down this hall. Follow me."

Once behind the office's closed door, Lance indicated a chair in front of his desk. "You have news about Penny?"

The officer sat with a weary sigh. "Perhaps, but let me start by saying I was on the phone with the investigators in

Maricopa County this morning. They located a body late yesterday and have identified it as the missing college girl. It's an apparent murder. They're doing an autopsy today."

Lance felt the color drain from his face. "She's dead? And she was connected to Penny somehow?"

"They were both at a party on New Year's Eve, just before the young woman disappeared."

"What tragic news for her family." Lance rubbed his brow. "And frankly, it makes me all the more worried about Penny. You mentioned that Penny's roommate saw her the next day, before she left campus to come here?"

"That's what she told the investigators."

"She should have arrived here by now."

"True. I looked into the details of your daughter's trip since we spoke yesterday. The bus line records show your daughter purchased a ticket late on Wednesday afternoon, New Year's Day. She was supposed to arrive here in Clearmont on Friday evening—actually, in the wee hours of Saturday morning. There were three transfers along the route where her ticket would have been scanned, but they only have scans of the first two. The last transfer should have happened in Barrett on Friday evening."

Lance's mind scrambled to calculate. "Friday? But this is Tuesday. Barrett is what … seventy, eighty miles from here? Where has she been all this time?"

Clemens nodded. "Good question. I drove over the pass to Barrett last night and talked to the bus station manager early this morning. At first, he couldn't offer much information. He said your daughter might have ditched her plans along the way. Apparently, it's not unheard of for people to buy a ticket and then not use it, or only go part of the distance."

Lance wrestled to grasp the implications. "So she might have changed her mind mid-trip? That's hard to imagine."

"It's one possibility, but there's also another. The station manager told me about an unusual incident that's connected to the bus that crashed on the mountainside Sunday night. He said some local gal he's acquainted with came into the bus station acting strange. She bought a ticket to Clearmont that night with cash."

"And *she* might be connected to Penny?"

"We haven't been able to determine that yet." Clemens scratched his head and shifted in his chair. "But the incident caught my attention because the station manager said she got on the bus without any luggage. That's when I realized *she* might be the Jane Doe up at the Wakeville hospital." He paused, his brows raised.

"Okay, but I still don't understand how that helps me find Penny."

"Well, he showed me her signature on the boarding manifest and told me the gal's name was Hope, but the signature is an initial P followed by a scribble that looks like it could be Penny."

Talk about a longshot clue. It was a triathlon away from conclusive. "You said the station manager knows this gal, so how could it be anyone else? And you still haven't explained why Penny would hang around in Barrett until Sunday night."

"I realize it's not all the answers we're looking for." Clemens leaned forward. "It's possible there's no connection at all, but I was hoping you might be willing to help me by looking at this patient up at Sierra Memorial. If nothing else, it might get us closer to determining this Jane Doe's identity."

Lance rubbed his chin. It wasn't the news he'd hoped for, but maybe he could help another family. "Sure, I'll help any way I can. Have you contacted the family of this other girl, Hope?"

"I've got some people checking into it."

"So, when do you need me to go?"

"If you have time right now, I could follow you up there."

"Sure, I'll make arrangements with Dr. Baird."

Before long, they were both on the road, Lance leading the way. After a forty-minute drive, they reached the picturesque mountain town of Wakeville, wedged in a crevice of intersecting canyons in Colorado's rugged high country. Lance's tires crunched over icy ruts left by the storm as he maneuvered through town and pulled into the hospital parking lot.

Sierra Memorial was a new facility and, though small, was well-equipped to serve their remote mountain region. Lance had met a couple of the doctors before and assured himself that if Penny were here, she would be getting quality attention.

Sergeant Clemens pulled into a space nearby and together they went inside to the information desk. After being directed to the third floor ICU, they got on the elevator.

Lance felt anxiety begin to rise as they approached the

ICU desk. A young woman in a lab coat looked up from a monitor as they stepped up to the nurse's station.

"Hello, I'm Dr. Doyle from Mercy Medical in Clearmont," He swallowed in an effort to calm the urgency in his voice.

"How can I help you?"

"I'd like to see the unidentified patient you have here from the bus crash."

She reached for a phone on the desk, "I'll contact Dr. Matheson for you. She's been taking care of her, and I believe she's still in the building."

"I just need to see whether or not I can identify the patient. It won't take long."

"Are you family?" She blinked as she realized her mistake. "Sorry, I automatically say that all day long."

"I understand. It's remote, but a possibility I could be family." He indicated the Sergeant standing behind him. "Also, this is Sergeant Clemens. He has another possible identity he's checking on."

"Of course." The nurse tapped information into her computer. "Were you aware the patient is on life-support?"

"No, but that's not surprising."

"If you'll allow me to get copies of your identification, I'll let you go ahead but, if you don't mind, only one of you at a time."

Clemens waved his hand and backed away. "You first. I'll be right over here." He indicated a small waiting area adjacent to the elevators.

The nurse entered more data in the computer and then stood and pointed down the hall. "She's in room 338, down this hall and around the corner to the left. I'll page Dr. Matheson, and ask her to meet you there."

"Thank you. That'll be fine."

Lance walked briskly down the hall, his stomach tightening with each step. At the door he hesitated. What if it *is* Penny? And what if Penny's injuries are beyond his ability to heal? That's how it had been with Marla's cancer. All his schooling, all his expertise—it had meant nothing in the face of that demon disease. If this is Penny…

Last night's group of faithful believers rushed to mind. Remembering how their prayerful petitions had filled him with fresh hope and strength to draw upon, he shut out the doubting voice in his head and prayed. "If it is her, Lord, help me. Help us both."

He opened the door. The bed, surrounded by equipment, first appeared unoccupied. Had the patient been taken elsewhere? The ventilator partially blocked his view. Its familiar rhythmic swishes added to the sounds of other monitors that blinked, hummed or clicked the recording of vital data.

He stepped closer, and glimpsed a mass of rumpled bedding and two arms lying limp on either side. Then the girl's face came into view—swollen in red and purple, with bandages covering her head. A tube tugged the corner of her mouth. Her lips, pale and chapped.

Could this be Penny? The girl seemed so small and helpless, more like a child than the energetic, willful young lady his daughter had grown into. How would anyone be able to recognize this girl in her present condition?

He maneuvered a monitor cart aside to approach the

bed. He could tell her hands were dainty in spite of being swollen with retained fluid. Tears brimmed his eyes. How could he be assured those pale curling fingers were Penny's? Had she ever worn such a garish shade of nail polish?

He wiped at his eye with a knuckle and focused on the distorted face, looking for familiarity in the contour of the girl's nose, and the long dark lashes lying against her purple cheek.

A sound at the door drew his attention. He turned to find a dark-haired woman in her mid-thirties at the door. The ID tag clipped to her lab coat identified her as the girl's doctor.

She stepped forward, extending her hand. "Dr. Doyle?" She had an accent—European of some sort, he guessed.

"Yes?"

"I'm Dr. Matheson."

She shook his hand, and Lance noticed a small silver cross necklace at her throat. "Pleased to meet you."

"I'm told you came in hopes of identifying our patient."

"I thought there was a possibility she was my daughter. This girl ..." He glanced back to the still form on the bed. "I thought sure I'd know immediately, but she's so badly bruised, so swollen."

"She had a bumpy ride, that's for sure. Five broken ribs, a broken collarbone, broken nose and cheekbone, and a nasty gash on the side of her head." She paused to inhale. "Her head injury is the most significant. We've had her on the ventilator since she arrived, but she's improved enough that we're preparing to wean her from it. If all goes well, she should be breathing on her own by morning." Dr. Matheson bent over the bed and lifted the blanket to put a stethoscope to her chest. After listening to heart and lungs for several seconds, she tucked the covers back in place. "All we know so far is that she's in her late teens or early twenties. She went through a rough patch initially—lost a lot of blood, but has remained stable for over twenty-four hours, so we're hopeful."

"Do you mind if I review her chart?"

"Of course not." She went to one of the carts, and logged into the computer. "This is it, right here." She stepped away from the monitor. "I'm sorry to hear your daughter is missing. I hope you're able to locate her soon."

She returned to the girl's bedside, while Lance scanned through the files. The X-rays and lab reports all looked as he expected. Penny had no birthmarks or tattoos he was aware of, so there seemed to be nothing of that nature to search. The notes indicated a couple partially healed bruises besides the ones from the crash, but nothing of obvious concern.

One thing that stood out was a graph of her brain activity. He pointed it out. "What do you make of this EEG?"

She glanced at it and nodded. "Yes, we noticed this on the initial round of tests when she was brought in from the crash site. I had our neurologist run new scans yesterday, and for some reason, the memory centers of her brain seem to rev up occasionally, becoming highly active for brief periods of time. Very unusual in a comatose patient."

Lance continued to flip through graphs and reports. Then he noticed the girl's blood type: O-Negative.

"See something else interesting?" the woman asked, pulling his attention away from the chart.

"It might not be anything, but this girl is O-Negative, like me."

Her dark brows rose. "A rare type—that's something."

Lance remembered the emergency blood donation he made yesterday. Perhaps it had been brought here for this patient. He left the computer cart and approached the bed again.

Leaning over the patient, he gently lifted an eyelid. Blue—as deep as the ocean. That's what he used to tell Penny about her eyes. He gently pulled back the edge of the bandage in front of her ear and saw the girl's dark copper hair lying in flattened waves beneath. Yes. Penny's hair. A flood of warmth surged through his body as his heartrate increased. Lifting the front edge of the bandage exposed a widow's peak on her pale forehead. Just like her mother's.

Penny. It couldn't be anyone else. Heat rushed up his neck, and he closed his eyes against a sudden welling of emotion. She'd been here, all alone for two days and he never knew it. How was that possible? He leaned against the bedrail for support as his knees weakened. *God, please,* he prayed silently, *I need another chance with my daughter. Take care of her, Lord. She's all I have left.*

THIRTEEN

Groaning, I slumped against the back wall of the consignment shop. "No. No, no."

Things couldn't have gone worse. My money, IDs, my phone, and of course, my suitcase too. They were all in Brock's car.

"Is something wrong, Miss?" The clerk eyed me from across the shop.

"Just all the important stuff." I returned to the front door, my shoulders slumped.

"If there's anything I can do…"

"I don't think so, but thanks."

Walking past her counter, I cracked open the door enough to peer through the glass toward Main Street. A couple pedestrians trudged the snowy sidewalks, but Brock wasn't among them. Not yet. In the other direction, cars filled most of the parking spaces. No people in sight. I sighed. Should I make a run for it? He could come around the corner at any moment—even while I leaned my head against the door.

The thought pulled me back, allowing the door to close.

"Are you sure you're all right?" The consignment lady leaned toward me with a concerned look.

What could I tell her? I searched for the right words. "I need … to…"

She tilted her head kindly and extended a hand toward me on the counter. "It's okay. Take a breath. You can tell me."

Part of me wished I could give up, go back and tell Brock I'd made a mistake. Promise to make it up to him somehow. Ask him to forget the note and go on as if my little meltdown hadn't happened.

But the vision of his face, twisted with rage, had made my blood go cold. It was the right decision, though it might be ill-timed. I couldn't go back, even though I'd always been the one to relent or apologize, whether I was right or wrong. Why hadn't I seen that before? Brock had never taken responsibility for anything. I always conceded. Always made allowances. With him, it would always be my fault.

"Miss?" The clerk's look hadn't wavered. "I'd be happy to call someone for you."

Did she mean the police? That seemed like an idea that could backfire big-time, since Brock had told them I fought with Abbi. Call Dad? How could I stir him into my troubles and hope to mend our relationship? "Thank you, but that won't be necessary."

"Are you sure?"

"Do you have a back door? I'd like to get to the bus station, but I'm trying to avoid someone."

She pulled back slightly. "Are you in some kind of trouble?"

"Just a guy. We broke up." A simplistic statement if ever there was one.

The clerk pulled her mouth to one side, thinking.

"Please? It would really help me out." I gripped my shoulder bag with sweaty hands.

"Well, there *is* an emergency exit in back. It goes out to a narrow walkway between the buildings."

My hopes rose. "That would be great."

"But the gates are locked at each end." She hesitated, her lips pursed. "I suppose I could let you out with my key. You'd come out close to the bus station."

"I'd appreciate that. Thank you so much." I pulled a smile across my clenched jaw.

The woman opened a drawer under the register and fished out a ring of keys. I followed her through a curtained area at the back of the store.

We went out the back door, and she led the way to a metal gate at the end of the passage. While she bent to fit the key in the padlock, I saw Brock's car parked across the street.

How had my life veered so far out of control? In the space of a few hours, we had gone from having a pleasant drive through the mountains to a Dear-John-style breakup and now, of all things, I was hiding from him.

I'd never recognized his dark moods and manipulations before. Others had. Cheri pointed out little incidents from time to time, and I had fluffed them off. No big deal. Now they glared at me.

How did other people manage break-ups? Maybe it was easier when they didn't involve the kind of accusations Brock had made today. If I were stronger, I could stand my ground in spite of how weak he made me feel. I would face him instead of hide.

But strength and assurance eluded me. Though I'd repeatedly insisted on my innocence, self-doubt, fueled by my memory lapses, had paralyzed my thoughts.

The clerk finally managed to free the lock and open the gate, which swung wide with a grating squeal. A chill wind gusted as I walked through to the sidewalk, so I zipped up the last few inches at the top of my coat.

"Thank you." It was all I could think to say as she hurried to lock the gate behind me.

The block was empty, my time limited. I hurried across the street and grabbed the rear door latch of Brock's car.

Locked.

My suitcase lay on the back seat in clear view; my phone and ID case were somewhere on the floor behind the front seats. So close. I tugged the driver's latch with the same result. With falling expectations, I moved to the back hatch. No luck.

Just one door. That's all I need, God.

I hurried to the far side of the car but, as usual, God hadn't heard me.

Biting my lower lip, I stared at the cold, gray sky. A snowflake landed on my face. Terrific.

I leaned forward, my forehead against the door glass. Were there any options left? I was out of ideas. Then, through the car windows, I saw someone march around the corner. Brock, hands rammed in his coat pockets, strode directly to the bus station. I dropped to crouch behind his car, thankful he hadn't looked my way. Then, rising slowly, I peeked around the metal pillar dividing the front and back windows. He was peering through the bus station window, his back to me. His shoulders dropped, he pulled out his phone, and turned around to face the SUV.

I pulled down to get my head below the windows. Was I fast enough? Eventually, I'd have to peek again, but how long should I wait? Could I see under the car? A quick glance told me, even with the higher clearance of 4-wheel drive, it wasn't feasible.

Then I heard footsteps crunching pebbles on the street as he approached the car. My heart raced. He would easily find me here, hiding from him, and I had no courage for a confrontation.

His footsteps stopped. He spoke to someone on the phone. "No, I've only started looking." The close proximity of his voice startled me. He must be standing right on the other side of the car.

"I'm not going through all that again with you, Tyler." His voice rose, clearly agitated. "Don't worry. I'll find her."

Brock's tone of voice made my insides clench. While he listened to the other side of the conversation, my heartbeat pounded like a drum in my ear. Though crouching nagged my sore hip, I didn't dare move for fear of being detected.

"Listen, I've done everything you asked, haven't I? Besides, I don't think she remembers anything, otherwise she'd run straight to the cops."

He's saying I would go to the police? He talked to the

investigators already—told them I fought with Abbi. Why would I go to the authorities if I remembered anything?

Then Brock shouted at his phone, making me pull my head lower. "She hasn't! Now stop worrying. I told you I would take care of her, and I will. I'll talk to you later." He kicked a tire for emphasis, and the car vibrated against my shoulder.

I'd never heard him so furious before. What would happen if I had to face him again?

More snowflakes fell, clinging to each other and swirling in the icy breeze. Brock clicked the door-lock button on his key fob and opened the driver's door. Was he about to drive away? Would he see me crouched on the sidewalk in his rear-view mirror?

He rummaged in the front seat and the glovebox for a minute, then got out and slammed the door. As he walked away, I exhaled a long-held breath. Leave it unlocked, I willed with my eyes pinched shut. I reached for the handle as he walked away, but the locks clicked before I lifted the latch.

When the horn chirped in acknowledgement, I wilted to the sidewalk. Nothing ever went right for me. I was on my own, and I needed a plan.

Falling snow continued to swirl under the gray skies, while I slumped against the car door, unable to coax myself out of the gloom.

Apparently, I was a problem—one Brock said he would "take care of." But what kind of problem could I be? My neck hairs stood on end. Was this the real reason why he drove so far to meet me at the inn? Why he questioned me? Why he pressured and argued?

Maybe he was trying to decide whether or not I remembered … whatever it was I was having trouble remembering. And it was something he believed would make me go to the police.

A shiver ran through me, but it wasn't the chill of the car door against my back. Maybe I should go to the cops, but what would I tell them? That I might be in danger? That I didn't know why? That something happened, but I couldn't remember it?

They might not throw me in jail—it would be a psych ward instead.

Where else could I get help? The consignment shop clerk had been sympathetic, but what could I ask of her?

I could ask for a place to hide. A place to tuck away until the evening bus.

What if Brock kept up his search all day? What if he were waiting at the bus station tonight? Would he let me get aboard? Would he make a scene by dragging me away to his car? And if he did, would anyone help me? The whole scenario sounded outrageous, but my panic refused to subside. Having overheard Brock's angry conversation with Tyler, the prospect of encountering him had only grown more ominous.

Rising slowly, I checked every direction. Brock was gone. I should have taken note of the direction he went, but maybe it didn't matter. I had to get back to the consignment shop.

I had nowhere else to go.

Taking a deep breath, I rushed around the car and crossed the street to the sidewalk. At the corner of the building I paused to breathe again.

Please don't let him see me.

Fighting against fear, I peeked around to the side street. *All clear.*

The consignment shop door was about fifty feet away, but my feet were frozen to the ice-crusted walkway.

No, they're not frozen. Quit stalling.

Another breath and I rounded the corner in a mad dash. Approaching the store's front window, Brock's harsh voice stopped me cold. I jerked back against the brick wall and pinched my eyes shut. *No, no, no!*

Another hard line from Brock. This one, I realized, was muffled. I couldn't catch the words. What's more, he wasn't talking to me, and he wasn't out on the sidewalk.

He was *in* the consignment shop.

FOURTEEN

W hat was Brock doing in the consignment shop? The brick wall snagged against my coat as I slid an extra inch away from the window.

Though his words were muffled, his voice commanded attention. The clerk's reply sounded high-pitched. Clipped. Was she frightened? Did I dare look in the window?

"Now! Right now!" Brock snapped clearly.

He must have moved close to the front of the store. Perhaps in front of the register, and if I were lucky, facing away from the window. Slowly, I leaned in from the side and saw them heading toward the back of the store. In a moment, they disappeared behind the curtain. She must be showing him how she'd helped me get away.

I didn't dare wait for their return. I took a quick breath, bolted past the windows and down the sidewalk.

Rounding the corner onto Main Street, I stopped and waited for my heart to slow. What now? In all likelihood, Brock would go from store to store asking where I could be found. He'd spin a tale so convincing, folks would eagerly become helpful informants. I'd seen that sort of thing in movies.

Was there any place he wouldn't look?

Maybe one. The place we had already been.

I looked toward the café. It was in the middle of the block—a few doors down from the corner where I stood. In fact, I could see their sign above the door—*Piece De Resistance*.

Another French business name. What were the odds of that? It struck me as amusing—and apropos, since I was "resisting" Brock. I smirked in spite of my distress.

Stepping away from the wall, I attempted a normal pace, taking slow breaths to stay calm. No sense flying through the door like a crazed woman.

The bell jangled as I entered. A majority of the lunch crowd had dispersed. I looked around for our waitress but didn't see her. Instead, a large, jowly woman called to me from behind the bakery counter. "Can I help you, miss?"

I navigated tables littered with dirty dishes to get to the counter. "Yes, I was here earlier, and the waitress was so kind. I wondered if maybe I could speak with her."

The woman eyed me up and down as if I'd asked for something that violated her principles. "Which waitress?"

"She's about my height with neon yellow hair."

"That would be Hope. I think she just clocked out." She went to the service door, cracked it open and hollered into the kitchen, "Is Hope still down here?"

Someone called back. "Yeah, hold on."

I stepped aside to let her help the next customer, and a few seconds later, the waitress came through the kitchen door.

Her face lit up when she saw me. "Hi." Her wide-eyed

surprise seemed enhanced by her electric-shock hair. She took my elbow and pulled me aside. "I didn't think I'd see you again. Boy, your guy sure got mad when he read that note."

"He's not my guy. At least, not anymore." Over Hope's shoulder, I saw the bakery counter woman scrutinizing us, so I edged a little farther away. "Sorry to put you on the spot, but I could really use your help again."

"How?"

"I need to be out of sight for a while. At least until he gives up and decides to leave town without me." I pinched my lips together and held my breath, hoping for an affirmative reply.

Hope's expression brightened immediately. "Oooo, sounds like espionage! I love it!" Her brown eyes gleamed. "And I have the perfect hiding place."

Relief washed over me. "Thank you so much." I glanced toward the front window, imagining Brock leaning in from the side, just as I had done at the consignment shop. We had no time to waste. "How soon can we go?"

"My shift is over. C'mon. You can hide in my apartment. I live right upstairs."

The bakery lady, packing a box of eclairs for a customer, kept her eye on us as Hope took me through the kitchen doors again.

I tugged her arm. "Do you think she'll tell Brock I'm here with you?"

"Celia? I doubt it. Besides, I don't think he'll come back."

"Why's that?"

"He left without paying the bill."

Whoa. I pulled back. Brock enjoyed waving around money when he had the chance. My departure must have shook him even more than I imagined. "Sorry. I'd be happy to pay you but my money is…"

Hope dismissed my concerns with a wave of violet-manicured fingers. "We'll worry about that later."

At the back of the kitchen, we exited into the same vestibule where Hope had shown me out the back door before. This time, though, we climbed narrow stairs in the opposite direction up to a landing flanked by two doors. She waved off the one on the left. "That's an old storage room, but *this*"—she swung the other open with a flourish—"is my humble abode."

Humble was putting it kindly. My new friend was apparently all about personality and rather little about housekeeping.

Straight ahead was a small kitchen with a breakfast bar, sink, stove, and counters, all buried under stacks of dirty dishes and the remnants of prior meal preparations. I forced my face to not react as I followed her in. She went to the sofa at the far end of the room and shoved aside piles of discarded clothing from the arms and cushions. A few hangers were strewn about too, which suggested her morning routine might consist of trying on everything she owned. The rest of the living area held a variety of less-distinguishable piles and stacks of boxes.

The sofa slumped in front of a wide bay window, the only source of natural light in this elongated multi-purpose room. A pair of mismatched armchairs sat at either side, burdened with books and papers. Behind me, a short hall led back from the entry door, undoubtedly to a bedroom and bath.

Once she'd cleared the sofa cushions, Hope knelt on them and pulled the curtains aside to widen the view. "Look. You can see all of Main Street from here."

Bracing my hands against the sofa back, I leaned toward the window. "You're right. This is so nice of you, Hope. I don't know how to thank you. I only wish I knew what to do next."

Hope propped her elbows on the sofa back and poised her chin in her hands. "Well first, you could tell me your name and why you're breaking up with that hunky guy."

Right. Hunky and dangerous. I straightened and pulled back from the sofa. "Sorry. I'm Penny Doyle from Clearmont."

"Hey, I've been to Clearmont before. Nice town." With a sudden jump-twist, Hope spun around, plopping onto the sofa cushion with a practiced finesse. She leaned to pat the cleared space beside her. "Have a seat."

"Thanks." I sat next to her and pulled my feet up under me, Indian-style, to avoid the floor piles. "I've been away at college in Arizona. I was heading home for a visit during semester break, but things have gotten complicated."

"Don't they always?" She matched my dismal tone, but then immediately popped up from the sofa and went to her refrigerator. "Want a soda? Or juice, maybe?"

Her quirky energy made me smile. "Sure, thanks."

"I'm sorta feeling like ... guava-pineapple. How about you?"

I giggled because she did a little shimmy in front of the fridge door when she said "guava-pineapple." Immediately, a strong wave of déjà vu washed over me once again. I had seen that shimmy before and giggled. I was sure of it.

Hope closed the refrigerator and stepped toward me. "Penny?"

"Huh?" My insides had begun to quiver, though the sensation was already fading.

"I've got some O.J. too, if you'd rather."

I couldn't tell her about the déjà vu. She'd think I was crazy... or crazier. "Guava-pineapple sounds great. Thanks."

She poured some into the last two glasses on the shelf beside the fridge and brought them over. "So..." She handed me one and held the other overhead while carefully wedging her narrow hips into a gap among the piles on the arm chair. "What happened between you and Mr. Wrong?" The book stack beside her teetered, so she propped her elbow on top. It kept her drink held high, as if she were posing for a regal portrait.

I pressed the rim of the glass against my chin a moment, inhaling citrus while I considered how much to tell. "We'd been arguing on the drive up here. That's all, really. I decided I'd rather go the rest of the way home on my own." I took a sip of the juice and licked my lips. "All I want now is to get on the bus going to Clearmont tonight. But Brock..." I stopped.

Telling more might cause the whole can of worms to gush out.

"Let me guess. Brock thinks he knows better than you."

Bullseye. She was right—at least partly. Except for the whole sordid tale of the missing student, the New Year's Party, the police investigators, the fight, my bruises and the lapses in my memory. That part was all too much, so instead of explaining, I nodded.

"But wait. That can't be the whole story." She leaned forward to study my face, leaving the stack of books beside her in peril. "Something's changed since you walked out during lunch. Now you're scared."

I bit my lips, and hot tears sprang out onto my cheeks. How could I tell her? "Really. I just need a place to stay until the bus arrives."

She nudged a pink slipper off a tissue box near her feet and pulled a couple sheets out to hand me. "Well, that's easy. You'll stay here." Taking a slow sip of her juice, she stared me in the eyes, then took a deep breath. "But you and I both know that might not be enough."

"No. Probably not."

Hope edged forward in her chair. The tower of books took on a Pisa-style slant when she reached out to place her free hand lightly on my knee. "Look, I realize it's not my business, but I'm ready to go all-in on helping you find a solution. Okay?"

I dabbed at my nose with the wadded tissue. "Thank you." Hope's offer might have sprung from her captivation with thrill-seeking adventures but, for the first time since leaving Brock, my growing anxiety receded a step.

Hope stood and set her glass on the chair arm. Pacing the room slowly, she tilted her head up and tapped her widespread fingertips together, like one of those TV detectives getting ready to announce the killer's identity. "So the situation, as I have gathered so far, is…" She spoke with an exaggerated air of affluence that reminded me of a British aristocrat, complete with hand flourishes. "We have an ex-boyfriend who isn't accustomed to being rejected. Am I right?" She didn't wait for an answer. "We also have a suitable escape route in mind which will be monitored by said ex-boyfriend. There is a solution, of course. We must focus our attention to think this through creatively." She paused to pick up her juice and took a regal sip. Finally, spinning toward me with dramatic flair, she resumed her own voice. "Did I mention I was a theater major?"

We both broke out in giggles.

Over the next half hour, I ended up telling her the whole sordid tale. She was a good listener, nodding and waiting patiently while I piled each layer on top of the previous one.

At the end, she said, "Wow. That's a lot to handle."

I looked aside. "Sorry to dump on you."

"No, that's okay. I just wish I had some pie to offer."

"What?"

She shrugged in answer to my surprise. "Pie fixes everything, you know."

"No, I didn't know that."

"Oh, yes. Everything." Her composure held momentarily, then burst into another giggle.

I wanted to laugh with her—pretend life was light and breezy. Like pie could cure everything. But that wasn't the truth, and I had to say it. "Too bad it can't solve this."

Hope took a breath. "Yeah, you're right. I get it." She took our empty glasses and added them to the pile in the sink. "So what do you think would solve it?"

Only one thing came to mind. "I have to find a way to get on the bus without Brock knowing." I leaned forward, resting my chin in my hands. "But how on earth do I accomplish that?"

We were both quiet for a moment. Then Hope's eyebrows rose. She pursed her lips and leaned back against the edge of the counter. "So… I have this idea…"

FIFTEEN

ope's idea involved transforming me into someone unrecognizable with the magic of theatrical wardrobe and makeup. The notion had merit, but as I surveyed the garment piles surrounding us, theatrical wasn't the first word that sprang to mind.

Hope must have seen my hesitation. She resumed her upper-crust accent and eccentric flourishes. "Oh ye of little faith. Follow me," she said, with a dramatic spin. Marching to the back of her apartment, she stopped at her bedroom door and flung it aside with a grand upswept gesture. "Ta-da!"

A glance inside revealed I'd been wrong about Hope keeping her entire wardrobe strewn over the sofa. She also had piles of clothes covering her bed, and an overstuffed closet had vomited even more onto the floor in front of its open door.

When we entered the room, a black cat emerged from under the bed, focusing on me with sparkling blue eyes.

Kitty? Was it possible? He hopped over a pile of jeans and drew his sleek back across my leg.

Hope was surprised enough to forget her accent. "Hey, he seems to already know you."

I crouched to pet him. "It's amazing. You won't believe this, but I could swear this is the same cat I met in Dalton a couple days ago."

"Really? This one attached himself to me while I was out shopping the day after Christmas." She kicked aside random discards as she made her way toward the closet pile. "He managed to get inside the apartment and I haven't had the heart to chase him off."

"The resemblance is amazing, that's for sure."

"He's really sweet, and I don't know … things just seem to be different around here since he showed up."

"Yeah, I know what you mean." I remembered Mrs. Wilton's comment about the cat being the hand of God.

"He seems to like it here, so I decided to name him Carlisle. What do you think?"

"Carlisle." I scratched behind his ears. "It's a respectable name. I like it."

Hope began to claw through the pile in front of the closet door. "I have an idea in mind. Give me a minute to find some things…"

Much later, after numerous wardrobe changes, I sat on a chair beside the bed in my "new" outfit, fanning my hands in order to dry the glittery turquoise nail polish Hope had applied. She, meanwhile, collected make-up from the adjoining bathroom. Carlisle nestled on a bed pillow monitoring our progress. The polish wasn't a shade I would have chosen, but Hope had insisted on it, mostly because she had some matching lipstick, if only she could locate it. She had been searching the cabinets for a couple minutes.

"Found it!" She appeared at the door holding up the tube, triumphant. "This is perfect. He'll never, ever recognize you."

I had to agree. Together with the goth-inspired "costume" she had assembled for me to wear and the jet-black, rock-star wig I hadn't yet had the courage to try on, I doubted I would even recognize myself.

Hope held out the bluish-green lipstick. "It's a great color as long as you don't get it on your teeth." I took it carefully, guarding my nails, and she shooed me to stand. "Go on. Have you even seen yourself yet?"

I walked over to the full-length mirror, and tried not to laugh. "I definitely don't look like me, that's for sure." I fingered the brass studded choker at my neck. "But what if this whole getup draws too much attention? Wouldn't it be better to wear something that would make me sort of 'invisible?' Someone not worth noticing?"

Hope's shoulders dropped. "You're right. You are *so* right." She resumed pacing again.

"Besides that, I have to travel on the bus in this—with other people. Maybe I could just be an ordinary person."

"Ordinary clothes… Hmmm. I might have some of those." She scanned the floor in front of the open closet again.

I twirled a stray curl at the nape of my neck, and an idea sprang to mind. "Or maybe an ordinary *pregnant* woman."

Hope's eyes flashed wide. "Oooo, I think I see where you're going with this."

"Yeah, I've heard guys ignore pregnant women. Brock might even look away."

More of the afternoon passed with a new round of Hope's ingenuity. At last, I stood before the mirror again wearing the black wig, newly *unstyled*, and layers of what Hope dubbed "Third Trimester Drab."

I had to admit, it looked pretty convincing.

"Okay, enough gawking." Hope lifted the wig off my head and placed it aside. "It's time for me to get dressed, so I can go get your ticket."

I changed out of the costume and into my own clothes. While she put the costume on and finished her makeup to match mine, I knelt on the sofa to watch out the window for any sign of Brock.

The sky had turned dark gray with the fading daylight. The temperature had dropped enough to crust the snow so it crunched under the passing cars below. With any luck, the deteriorating weather had encouraged Brock to leave town. I hated the thought of abandoning my stuff in his car, but we hadn't been able to come up with a plan to retrieve it. It was something I'd have to sort out after all the craziness settled down.

Hope came out of the bedroom. "Well, what do you think? Is the wig straight?"

She really looked pregnant. I stared, my mouth agape, as the reality of our plan sunk in. "I can't believe we're really doing this."

"Why not?"

"I wouldn't have been able to come up with a plan, let alone have the means to accomplish it. Not without your help. If the tables were turned, and you'd been the one coming to me—"

"You would have done whatever you could."

"I don't even have money to repay you for buying my ticket."

"You'll repay me when you can. It's fine." She stepped forward, her eyes deflecting my concerns. "Don't worry, Penny. This is going to be fun. I'm an actress, remember?"

"But you might run into Brock. What will you do then?"

"So what? It's not like he's searching for *me*. Besides, if he gets a good gander now, he'll be even less likely to pay attention when he sees you in this get-up later."

"Good point." Once again I made an internal resolution not to worry.

We wrapped her coat the best we could around her pillow-enhanced body, and soon she was out the door.

I paced the apartment, while Carlisle monitored my zigzags from the back of the sofa. When I finally sat, he hopped to the cushion beside me, and I drew him to my lap.

I closed my eyes. "Please, please God." I whispered the words without thinking, and then shook my head when I caught myself. *Don't be silly. Prayer is like talking to the wind.* Setting Carlisle aside, I stood and circled the perimeter of the living room, rubbing the nervous tension from my arms. "I just want to be home."

If Mom were there, she'd open the door, and her eyes

would widen with surprise, crinkling at the corners. She'd throw her arms around me with repeated squeezes while speaking my name against my neck. She'd draw me inside to the warmth of the front room, where she often kept a fire during winter months.

But why torture myself with such thoughts? Mom wouldn't be there.

In my mind's eye, I stared at the front door, waiting for it to open. What would Dad do? The door didn't move. I couldn't visualize it without Mom on the other side.

Tears sprang to my eyes again, threatening to ruin my makeup. I wanted to see her so much, but instead, Dad *was* on the other side.

I shook the negativity from my shoulders. What was I thinking? Dad was a caring man too. People always spoke well of him. "Dad, will you be there for me?" The words came without prompting. "I really need you."

"Penny?"

What was that? A faint voice, distant but clear.

"Penny, I hope you can hear me." It was Dad's voice coming to me from far away. Was he standing out on the street?

I rushed to the window and scanned the snow-crusted sidewalk below. "Dad?" I wiped my eyes, smearing mascara on the back of my hand.

"Penny." His voice seemed to waver in the air like the gently swirling snowfall. Distant, yet tender, even plaintive.

"Daddy?"

"Hold on sweetie. Everything will be okay."

SIXTEEN

L ance was overcome with emotion as he leaned over the still form on the bed. His only child had returned, yet still she remained so far away. Why hadn't he tried harder to draw her back home at Christmas? He blinked and a tear fell to her swollen, purple cheek.

"Penny?" His voice was barely above a whisper. "Penny, can you hear me?"

No sign of response.

"Penny, I'm here. It's Dad." He took hold of her hand. So cool to the touch. "I'm sorry I wasn't here sooner, but I'm here now. Hold on, sweetie. Everything will be all right."

He sensed Doctor Matheson draw near. She lay her hand gently on his shoulder. "We've been easing back on the meds today in order to begin weaning her from the ventilator. She'll gradually get closer to consciousness and become more aware of voices. I'm glad you're here to help guide her back."

"I should have been here sooner."

"You're here now. That's what's important." She maneuvered through the equipment toward the door.

"Stay as long as you like. I need to finish my rounds, but I'll be back in the morning. If you need anything at all, just let the charge nurse know."

"I won't be going anywhere."

Soon after she left, however, Lance remembered Sergeant Clemens. He needed to go back to the waiting area. Reluctantly, he laid Penny's hand on the blanket and left her room.

As Lance walked up the hall, he noticed Clemens paging idly through a magazine in the waiting area. In a seat nearby, a young man with dark hair seemed to be studying the officer. Clemens caught Lance's approach and stood, causing the other fellow's gaze to flash upward. His face seemed to register recognition before quickly shifting away to study the phone on his lap.

Who was this guy?

Clemens drew his attention with a questioning look. "You took some time in there. Is she—?"

Lance coughed and nodded discretely in the young man's direction. "Could you come with me, please?"

Clemens caught the signal. "Of course."

Lance led the way to an area behind the elevators. "Maybe I'm letting my imagination get away from me, but that young man seemed keenly interested in our conversation."

"Hmm, I hadn't noticed." He patted Lance's back. "Don't worry too much about it. Curiosity is pretty typical."

Lance rubbed his brow. "I suppose you're right. I keep

thinking about Penny's possible connection to the missing college student. It's got me on edge."

"That's understandable. What about the Jane Doe?"

"I would have wagered against it, but your instincts were right. My daughter *is* in that room." Lance paused a moment when his voice cracked with emotion. "She's hardly recognizable."

"I'm sorry to hear that, doctor, but glad we both know where she is. Will she be okay?"

Lance nodded. "Fortunately, her condition's stable. The doctor believes she's ready to wean off the ventilator."

"That's good. And now you can be here when she wakes. I'll contact Maricopa County and let them know we've located her. They'll probably send someone up to interview her."

"I doubt she'll be doing any interviews soon. There are plenty of questions, though. Like why she boarded that bus under a false name."

"And why the station manager identified her as someone he knows."

Lance drew his hand across the back of his neck. "I guess we'll know more when Penny revives. Thanks for your efforts, sergeant."

Clemens checked his wristwatch. "I need to leave, but I'll pass along the info about your daughter's situation and see how they decide to proceed." He paused to look Lance in the eye. "Are you doing okay?"

"Sure." It wasn't entirely true. "What I mean is, I'm better knowing where Penny is, but this whole situation with the murdered girl..." He rubbed a hand along his clenched jaw.

The worry lines on Clemens brow softened. "Let me handle that while you take care of your daughter."

"You're right." At the moment, what else could he do?

After Clemens left, Lance phoned his pastor. "Mark? I've found Penny."

"That's good news. Thank you, Lord."

"Yes, good—and not so good. She's at Sierra Memorial. She was on that bus, Mark. The one that rolled over up on the pass."

"What?"

"Remember when I mentioned they had a Jane Doe patient here?"

After explaining the details to Mark, Lance called his office to let them know he would stay at Penny's bedside overnight. Another call updated Dr. Farthing and the staff at the surgical ICU.

He tucked his phone away, and noticed darkness outside the window at the end of the hall. Winter's brief daylight hours were already gone. Perhaps he'd get a bite to eat before returning to Penny's room.

He headed back to the elevators. Rounding the corner, the dark-haired young man sitting in the waiting room looked up. "Sir?" He rose from his seat, his expression earnest. "May I speak with you?"

He was tall, six-one or two, by Lance's estimation. Around Penny's age, perhaps. "Have we met?"

"No, sir, but I know your daughter. You're Dr. Doyle, right?"

Lance's inner senses prickled. "Yes."

"I thought so. Penny showed me a photo of the two of you taken at her graduation."

"You from around here?"

"No sir. Penny and I met at Hillman Oaks. I drove up in hopes of seeing her."

From the college? Five hundred miles away? Lance shifted his stance. "How did you learn she was here?"

"I, uh, heard from her while she was traveling and..." He bit his lip, eyes darting aside. "When I figured out she was on the bus that crashed, I came as soon as I got the news."

Lance crossed his arms. Her identity hadn't been known until now. Why was this guy lying? "Look, what did you say your name was?"

"Brock Harper." He straightened and offered a handshake. "Perhaps your daughter has mentioned me? We've been dating since about Thanksgiving."

"Brock." Lance gave Brock's hand a single definitive shake. "I'm heading down to the cafeteria for something to eat. Perhaps you'd let me buy you some supper. That way, we could talk a bit. Get acquainted."

Brock glanced down the hall toward Penny's room, then back. "Umm, sure. That'd be great. Thanks."

Lance punched the call button for the elevator, while considering the young man. From what he remembered of Penny's high school beaus, this guy would fit her idea of handsome, but those chiseled features and air of respectfulness hid something bothersome. Something further aggravated by the knowledge he had lied.

Brock swiped a hand over his hair, perhaps to smooth some nervous tension. "I'm glad I ran into you." The elevator opened and they got on. "I've been eager to see Penny, to make sure she's okay."

"I'm afraid she's not in a condition to have visitors yet." Lance punched the button for the mezzanine level.

Brock nodded. "I understand. I wouldn't want to disturb her. Just sit there, you know. Let her know I'm here."

Lance nodded. "Have you spoken to her roommate?"

Brock stuck his hands in his pockets. "Cheri? No. Not yet. I suppose I should do that."

"If you have her number handy, I would like to give her a call too."

"Sure." His words were agreeable, but he made no move to deliver on the request.

The elevator stopped and they stepped out to find the cafeteria across the hall. After getting in line, they each selected a dinner entree and found seats at an unoccupied corner table.

Brock took a bite from his hamburger immediately, while Lance smoothed a napkin over his lap and bowed his head for a momentary grace. When he finished, Brock seemed to have paused mid-chew to watch.

Lance ignored the stare. "Tell me, Brock, I'm curious about how you and Penny met."

Brock finished chewing and swallowed. "Umm. There's not much to tell, really. I'm a wide receiver with the Hillman Panthers, and Penny's roommate is a cousin of one of the linebackers. She introduced us after the division game the weekend before Thanksgiving."

"So, you've only known each other a few weeks?"

"Yeah, but she's a terrific girl." He took a swig from his drink. "I can see us being together a long time."

Lance nodded. "Did Penny tell you why she decided to come home?"

Brock took a big breath while wiping his mouth with a napkin. "Homesick, I guess. It's a shame about the bus accident. She'll recover though, right?"

"It's going to take time. Probably some physical therapy. She may not be back at school for a while." Lance took a bite of pot roast while pondering how to get more information. Then again, maybe that wasn't possible, since Brock liked to play loose with the facts.

Brock salted his fries. "She have any broken bones?"

Lance sliced a chunk of potato on his plate. "A few. Her head injury has been the main concern, but the doctors have been keeping close watch on her."

"So, you're not her doctor? Penny said you were a surgeon, so I assumed…"

"She's in capable hands. I'm happy to just be her dad right now." He lifted the napkin to wipe his mouth.

Brock chewed awhile, apparently deep in thought. "Head injuries are tough, man. She could have, like, memory issues or something, right?"

For some reason, the question seemed loaded with hidden meaning. What was this guy getting at? "That's possible, but many patients experience no long term difficulties if their recovery is well-managed. That's why we're hopeful." Lance lifted a forkful of salad. Time to get the subject back on Brock. "So, tell me more about yourself, Brock. Where are you from?"

Brock kept his eyes on his plate. "California, originally."

"Your family still there?"

"Yeah."

"You like it at Hillman?"

He glanced up and nodded. "It's been all right. I went for the football program."

"I seem to recall the Panthers came out as division champions."

Brock pulled his shoulders back and smiled. "So, you've heard about my man, Tyler Williams, then?" He wagged his head in admiration. "That guy's a phenom' on the field. I've been his wide-receiver all through school. We're known as the Dynamic Duo."

Lance nodded without comment.

"Yeah. We've been great friends, both on and off the field, and now…" He raised his hands to sight-in with an imaginary rifle. "Pow. We're homing in on the draft. Gonna go pro this year."

Lance swallowed. "Congratulations. Looks like you guys have put Hillman in the news."

Brock nodded agreement, but something in his expression changed. Maybe something to do with Hillman's other news.

Lance tested the subject. "Speaking of news, I hear there's a girl from Hillman who turned up missing recently. You know anything about it?"

Brock had picked up some fries from his plate, but at this, he set them aside. "Only what the news reports said a couple days ago." He rolled the edge of the napkin beside his plate.

"So maybe you haven't heard. They found her body." Lance studied his face. "She's been murdered."

Brock picked up his burger without reaction. "Sounds like you know more than I do."

"I was curious whether you or Penny might know this girl."

"Penny might have known her."

"But not you?"

"Oh, I don't know." He took a bite and chewed. "We may have met. Hillman's not a big campus."

Lance straightened in his chair and took another forkful of pot roast. That cool demeanor made him uneasy, and his instincts were flagging against further pursuit of the subject. Clemens might be interested in talking with this guy, and in the meantime, it might be best not to give him reason to clam up entirely.

SEVENTEEN

"You should have seen the look on his face." Hope stood inside her apartment door and held out the bus ticket toward me, a wide smile across her face. "It was priceless."

"You saw Brock?" I took hold of the printed stub, sandwiching it between my hands.

"No, not him." She pulled off the wig and loosened her neon hair with a rake of her hand. "I'm talking about Sean, the bus manager. When I waddled in, his eyes got big as saucers. I told him I was trying out a costume for a new role." She giggled, tossing the wig on the sofa, where it resembled a deflated Carlisle. "He remembered me playing Rizzo in *Grease* last year, so—"

"But was Brock there?"

"Yeah, but not at first. He walked in a couple minutes later. By then, I'd already told Sean I was researching a role as a runaway maternity patient." She removed her coat. "Good, huh? Sean doesn't know anything about theater, so he just went along with everything I said."

"Was Brock paying attention to your conversation?"

Hope flung her coat over a chair back and it slowly slid

to the floor. "Don't worry. He didn't hear the part about me playacting, but he probably heard stuff after that."

"Like what?"

She patted my arm. "Like I said, don't worry, Penny. I think this plan will work. I even signed in for you, so you won't have to go inside the station. When I was leaving, Brock was standing by the door and he opened it for me. I looked right at him and thanked him, so now he associates my face with 'the pregnant girl.' You shouldn't have any trouble at all."

She pulled off her boots and plopped onto the sofa next to the wig. I picked it up so I could sit too. "I wish I had your confidence. It all seems scary to me."

Hope leaned sideways, examining my face. "What happened to you?"

I'd forgotten the mascara streaks. "You're going to think I'm crazy, but weird things are happening to me. While you were gone, I could swear I heard my dad's voice for a while. I thought he was outside, trying to talk to me."

She put her arm around my shoulder with a squeeze. "You're weird, but that's cool. Soon you'll be home, and everything will be fine."

I lowered my gaze. "I hope so. Dad and I haven't gotten along so well since Mom died."

"How old were you when that happened?"

"Sixteen."

Hope pulled back with a pat to my arm. "I'm sure you've both changed since then."

"Yeah, I guess."

She was right. We had struggled, but that didn't mean we always would. We both had changed. Hearing his voice, even in my imagination, had fueled my desire to get home. I needed family, and for the first time, it seemed my ache about Dad might actually be yearning instead of worried frustration.

Hope was hungry so we rummaged in the fridge, and after eating a snack, I put on the pregnancy costume. She worked her magic once again with my makeup. When I finally donned the wig and stood in front of the mirror, I didn't see myself at all.

Hope fussed with the back of the wig where it lay over my collar. "You'll have to let me know how all this works out."

"Sure. Write down your number."

Before we knew it, the time had come to leave. I put Hope's phone number in my coat pocket along with the ticket, and left her apartment just before nine o'clock. I walked to the side street trying to appear leisurely. When I reached the far corner of the consignment store building, I waited for the bus, grateful to have an inconspicuous vantage point. Temperatures had dropped well below freezing since nightfall, but the pregnancy pillow and extra layers kept me warm.

Soon the bus came up the street and rounded the corner where I stood. It pulled in front of the station's big plate-glass windows, where light spilled onto the walkway. A wave of panic seized me. Brock could be watching from inside those windows. And in the light that spilled onto the sidewalk, he would be able to see me clearly.

Hope's plan suddenly seemed to border on insanity. What were we thinking? Even more, what could I do when he saw through my ridiculous costume?

The driver stepped down from the bus door and went inside with a clipboard of papers. I swallowed my fears repeatedly while waiting for him to return. After a minute he did, and I took a deep breath. I rounded the corner and put on my best impression of confidence while marching up the block.

Brock or no Brock, this was it.

A couple people exited the bus and paused to speak with the driver while I walked their way. When they went inside the station, the driver noticed my approach. "Can I help you, ma'am?"

I attempted a smile and pulled the ticket from my pocket. "Here you go." The light of the station window seemed like a spotlight. I trembled at the exposure. Was Brock watching? I didn't dare look. A knot caught in my throat, and I shifted my position subtly toward the bus to minimize my facial profile.

"No luggage, ma'am?"

His question jolted me. I swallowed the knot and took a breath. "No. I'm only going as far as Clearmont."

He studied the ticket. "I see. Do you have your ID handy?"

"My… ID?" I choked and covered my mouth. "I… uh." I groped in my bag as if to search, knowing full well I couldn't produce anything that would work.

The bus station door behind me creaked open, and my heart rate shot up. Was Brock coming outside? I froze, unable to breathe. An unfamiliar voice called, "Hey, Hope. What day did you say you were coming back?"

Though it wasn't Brock, I didn't dare turn my head. What was the ticket guy's name? I couldn't remember. I lifted my shoulder for cover and turned my face ever so slightly. "Tuesday," I called out with a cough, hoping he wouldn't notice my voice, which sounded nothing like Hope's.

The driver scanned my ticket's barcode. "You know this lady, Sean?"

"Oh sure. But don't believe everything you see. Hope's always playacting something." He laughed aloud and I heard the door close.

The driver handed back my ticket. "Looks to me like you're good to go."

I climbed the bus steps and discovered more people onboard than I'd expected. Toward the back, I chose a pair of vacant seats on the side opposite the station window. While I crammed my coat into the overhead bin, I saw Brock's SUV across the street. Its presence taunted me with thoughts of my suitcase, my phone and ID—all so close, yet hopelessly out of reach.

When I turned to sit down, I caught sight of Brock through the opposite window, and my heart skipped. He had come outside the station door and was looking down at something on the sidewalk. He stooped to pick it up—a scrap of pink paper.

Hope's name and phone number. It must have slipped

out of my pocket when I pulled out the bus ticket. He looked it over, then glanced up to scan the dark-tinted bus windows. My mouth went dry. Could he see me?

He started toward the bus door and the driver stopped him. By Brock's hand gestures, I could tell he intended to come aboard. I looked around, desperate. The only place to hide was in the bathroom at the back of the bus.

I maneuvered down the aisle as fast as my pillow-wrapped tummy would allow and locked myself into the cramped cubicle, uncertain what to do next. Minutes passed while I studied my worried face reflecting back from the vanity mirror.

A soft knock on the door disrupted my thoughts. "Are you okay, Miss?"

"Yes, almost done."

I smoothed the wig and tried to swallow my panic. The bus lurched, pulling away from the curb as I slid the door open and scanned the back of the passengers' heads. Brock was not among them.

A guy in the back row beside me looked up. "I'm glad you're all right. I was starting to wonder if you were going to give birth in there." He chuckled and I attempted a smile before navigating back to my seat.

Sitting heavily, I exhaled a sigh. Soon I would be home. Once again, I envisioned walking up the driveway and through the arbor to the entry alcove. Surrounded by a hedge of boxwoods, Mom's potted flowers always filled the space with fragrance and color, and the small café table and chairs positioned beside the door added a sense of welcome. When I imagined pressing the door buzzer, I took a deep breath. A moment later, Dad opened the door, but the expression on his face made me step back. His brow creased with unspoken sorrow—the same look I'd caught sight of when my grandpa remarked how much I had grown to look like Mom. He'd nodded with an expression that made it clear I'd become a reminder of his greatest loss.

A woman with a baby on her lap, leaned toward me from across the aisle. "When are you due?" Her voice startled me back to the rocking jostle of the bus.

I hadn't prepared an answer. "Oh … umm … in a few weeks, I guess."

She nodded. "Ah, no wonder you had to travel by bus."

"Well, I'm only going as far as Clearmont."

"I see. Well, that's a short trip." Her baby cried, drawing away her attention.

I settled back into my seat with a sigh. Against all odds, Hope's plan had worked. In about three hours I would be in Clearmont, and now that I'd gotten away from Brock, he would have to accept the finality of our relationship and head back to Hillman.

Of course, that wouldn't solve all my problems, but it would be a good start at getting my life back to normal.

EIGHTEEN

Lance checked his watch—8 a.m. Two hours since the ventilator had been removed. Fortunately, Penny's breathing and vitals were holding. A slight twitch had recently begun in the corner of her eye, evidence of a REM sleep pattern. He took it as a sign she was edging closer to consciousness.

He lifted her limp hand and held it between his own. "Penny. Do you know I'm here?" He stared at her lashes. Two little tremors at the corner of her eye, then after three or four seconds another small twitch. "Don't you worry about a thing, sweetie. I'm going to be right here when you wake up."

A light tap at the door drew his attention. Dr. Matheson entered with a sheaf of papers and a smile that brightened the room. "Good morning. Looks like your daughter has managed the transition off the ventilator nicely."

Her accent, which he'd learned was Italian, made him smile. "I agree. They reduced the machine to fifty percent around midnight, and she sailed through the next six hours without a hitch. She's still doing great since they shut it off."

Dr. Matheson held out the papers. "Her vitals have remained consistent. Everything's looking very positive. I'll put in an order to have the trach removed this morning and, if all goes well, we might see her emerge from this coma late this evening or early tomorrow."

Lance accepted the papers, though he already knew the results from his own overnight monitoring. "Thank you."

"You're quite welcome." She smiled. "I'll check back later this afternoon. Until then, *ciao*."

He glanced at the papers, yawning. After little more than brief dozing through the night, he needed coffee and a toothbrush. Shaving would be a good idea too.

Fortunately, his cordless shaver was still tucked into the glove box of the car. Since Penny was doing so well, he could probably slip out and take care of that.

On his way to the elevator, his phone rang. Pastor Mark. "Hey, good morning, Mark. How are things in God's country?"

Mark chuckled. "Fine, I guess. I put Penny on the prayer chain last night."

"Great. God's already begun answering those prayers." He reached the elevator and punched the call button. "They weaned Penny from the ventilator last night, and I think she's showing signs of returning to consciousness."

"Thank you, Jesus." Mark cheered.

"Amen." Lance's heart warmed at having openly acknowledged God's goodness.

"Listen, I have some time available this morning. I'd like to drive up, maybe pray with you both."

Lance glanced through the windows of the adjacent waiting area. "Looks like a good day for traveling up the canyon. The sun's out, so maybe those slushy roads will clear."

"Great. I'll see you soon."

Lance took the elevator down and went out to the parking lot, found his car and rummaged in the glove box for the shaver. Sitting in the passenger seat, he tilted down the visor mirror. As he finished, a dark SUV pulled into a spot in the row behind him. It looked a lot like the SUV that had parked in front of his house. A young man in jeans and a black sweatshirt climbed out, removed his baseball cap and tossed it inside. It had to be the same guy who'd been parked by his house.

The man locked his SUV and glanced around before heading toward the hospital door.

Lance's heart skipped at seeing the man's face— Penny's boyfriend.

He waited until Brock entered the building before getting out of his car, then went to the SUV and checked the license plate. It matched his memory of the one that had been parked near his house. That meant Brock was in Colorado at least a day earlier than he'd let on, but why? And why set up surveillance?

Lance went inside, but Brock had already left the foyer, undoubtedly on his way to the third floor ICU. Lance took the stairs, his pulse quickening. At the second floor he slowed his pace, hoping for inspiration on what his best course of action should be.

Reaching the third floor, he stepped out to a corridor behind the elevator and whispered a quick prayer. *Lord, guide my actions and words.* A flurry of options blurred his thoughts. Should he confront Brock? What answers could he hope to get? He rounded the corner and saw Brock at the end of the hall, talking to a nurse at the ICU desk. Something in the young man's posture didn't sit well. He was quizzing the receptionist; either that or pressuring her somehow. She glanced Lance's direction and waved him over.

"Dr. Doyle," she said, when he reached the desk. "This young man has requested to visit your daughter, but I see that her chart currently indicates 'family members only.' If you would like to—"

"That's correct." Lance cut in. "Family members only. Pardon the intrusion, but I would like to speak privately with Mr. Harper." He looked Brock in the eye and nodded toward the empty waiting area. "If you'll step this way."

Brock's eyebrows raised. "Mr. Doyle … I mean, Dr. Doyle. You won't let me visit Penny? I drove all this way to see her—to be a help to her, if I can."

"Right now I need you to be a help to me."

Brock's eyebrows rose. "How?"

Lance gestured again to the waiting room. After Brock took a seat, Lance pulled another chair over to sit opposite him. "You can start by telling me in detail, just how you came to know that Penny was hospitalized here."

"It's like I said yesterday—"

"No. It's not."

Brock's eyes blinked twice, his mouth open, before

speaking again. "Okay, maybe I oversimplified a bit, but—"

"That's why I'm asking, Brock. I'd like a clear picture."

"Yeah, okay."

Lance leaned forward, propping his arms on his knees. Brock sat back, his brows angling defensively. "I'm not sure what you want to know."

"Everything. Details."

Brock stared back, his mouth working as if chewing his tongue, but he didn't speak. Lance waited, forcing his expression to remain neutral. Perspiration began to show on Brock's forehead and he scratched his neck. "I first talked to Penny while she was traveling."

"What day was that?"

His eyes shifted to the side. "Umm ... had to have been Thursday or Friday. Thursday, I guess." He nodded.

"What did you talk about?"

"Nothing special." He shrugged. "A little about school ... and why she decided to leave on this trip."

"Okay. What did she say about that?"

Brock bit his upper lip. "She regretted not going home for Christmas. She wanted to patch things up with you."

This was unexpected. A knot formed in Lance's chest and his mouth went dry. "Thank you. I didn't know that. Did you talk with her any other time?"

"On... uh, Saturday. I thought she was at your place, but she said she missed a connection and was waiting for the next bus."

"What happened after that?"

"I don't know. She didn't answer my calls anymore.

When I heard about the bus rolling off the mountain, I decided to drive up here."

"How did you know she was on that bus?"

"The last time I talked to her, she told me what bus she was planning to take." Brock draped his arm on the back of the chair next to him. "Look, are you going to allow me to see Penny or not? I came here to help, but I can just as easily leave you guys to work things out on your own."

Lance wasn't impressed. The kid dodged back and forth between nervousness and defensive leveraging in the space of a few minutes and over a few simple questions. Something was up, and he didn't like the feeling in his gut when it came to this guy. Still, he didn't want to run him off either. Not if there might be a way to get more information. At the very least, he hoped to get Officer Clemens' assessment of the guy. "Okay, let's go see Penny."

"Both of us?"

"Yeah, I'll let you spend some time with her, but I'm going to be with you both the whole time."

"Sure, fine." Brock shrugged and got up from the chair. "Right now?"

"Right now."

They went down the hall to Penny's room. Some of the monitors had been removed overnight, and since the ventilator disconnection, it had been pushed back against the wall. While he'd been out shaving, the trach tube had also been removed. A strip of gauze was now taped across Penny's neck.

Brock paused at the door before approaching her bed,

probably taken aback by the extent of her injuries. Lance leaned against the door frame and felt a fresh pang of regret at seeing her desperate condition. Was it true she had returned to Colorado in hopes of patching things up with him? At the very least, her bruises and subsequent swelling were the result of trying to get home. If only he'd known how to be the kind of father she needed, perhaps this whole scenario could have been avoided.

Brock stepped up to the bed and took hold of Penny's hand. Leaning over her, he whispered while his thumb caressed the top of her fingers.

Lance's phone chirped, indicating a new text from Officer Clemens. ARE YOU AT SIERRA MEMORIAL? I HAVE NEW INFO.

He keyed a quick reply. YES. COME ANY TIME. NOW WOULD BE IDEAL.

He hit "send" and looked up. Brock had straightened his back, but he still stood beside Penny's bed holding her hand. Lance noticed her fingers flexed rigid. Then they gripped Brock's.

"What's happening?" Lance said, rushing forward.

Brock dropped her hand and backed away. "I don't know. Is she waking up?"

Lance reached for Penny as her head tilted back and her back arched. Her mouth gaped and her body tensed. The ICP monitor began to beep, and was faintly echoed by a companion alarm at the nurse's station down the hall.

Lance turned to the monitor. "Her pressure just spiked. What happened, Brock?"

"I swear, man. I don't know."

"Move back."

He complied as Lance shifted his attention to Penny and lifted her eyelids. Unequal dilation. Other monitor alarms kicked in, as she began to tremble. The symptoms indicated neurological trauma—the implications critical. He had no stethoscope, so he leaned over her, pressing his ear to her chest, as medical personnel rushed in.

"Possible cerebral hemorrhage," Lance called as they surrounded the bed.

One young man grasped his arm. "If you'll step aside, please." Others called out instructions as they opened supply packs and keyed orders into their equipment.

Lance tugged his arm free. "She's my daughter."

"I understand, sir—"

His voice raised a pitch. "I'm a doctor."

"So am I, sir. I'll take good care of her. Right now, you be her dad." He shifted his attention to the other techs. "Get her to CT. I'll call it in."

Lance stepped back and willed the tension in his arms to ease. The young doctor was right. In this all-too-familiar situation, the team needed to work without distraction. Had their roles been reversed, he would have given the very same orders.

"Let's move it," a technician called to the response team.

Already in high gear, the group accelerated to meet the challenge.

A sound behind Lance caught his attention. Looking over his shoulder, he saw Pastor Mark standing just outside the doorway, wide-eyed. "I just got here. What's happening?" His eyes scanned the bustle of activity.

Lance glanced back to the frenzy of technicians surrounding Penny's bed and shook his head. "I think she's having a stroke, Mark. We have to pray."

NINETEEN

I dreamt I was back at the New Year's Eve party.

Tyler clapped and whistled with glee while his girlfriend swayed in the middle of the living room to sultry jazz music. Abbi's flapper-style dress glittered in the room's low light; the fringe on its hem slapping her thighs in rhythm with the drum beat. I glanced toward Brock who sat beside me, also focused on the spectacle. His arm draped the back of the sofa behind me, his hand caressing my shoulder, but his mind was clearly a million miles away.

I scanned the room looking for a diversion. Another couple sat in chairs opposite us. The guy nodded appreciatively toward Tyler, as if in gratitude for the evening's entertainment, while his date, a girl whose name I had already forgotten, wiggled and giggled in her seat, waving her arms like a hula girl. Definitely too much to drink.

A fourth couple stood in the doorway to the kitchen, engrossed in private conversation, though his eyes occasionally strayed to Abbi's performance. He was a cowboy with a strong Texas drawl, and she was someone

I'd met at a lecture on Synthetics a couple of months earlier. We had spent time renewing our acquaintance over hors d'oeuvres, and laughing over remembrances from the lecture.

She wasn't laughing now. Their whispered confidences seemed very serious.

The song ended and Abbi caught our attention with a dramatic swooping bow while simultaneously scooping my drink up from the coffee table. "Delicious," she declared, holding the glass toward Tyler. Was she referring to him or the drink? I raised my hand, but she downed it before I could tell her it was mine.

Brock leaned over and kissed my cheek. "Don't worry, babe. I'll get you another."

He stood and moved toward the kitchen, interrupting the serious couple's conversation.

The guy tapped Brock's shoulder as they parted to let him by. "I think we're going to head out a little early, if y'all don't mind."

"Oh?" Abbi spun their way with a pout and nearly lost her balance. "Don't go." Her head bobbled. She was very drunk.

My lecture-mate ignored Abbi, but gave Tyler a nod. "Thanks for inviting us." She set her glass on the coffee table. "I hope you and Brock both do well in the draft."

I scooted to the edge of the sofa. "Let me get your coats." When I got up, however, the room tilted and bile rose in my throat. I inhaled sharply as the carpet seemed to be pulled from under my feet.

A sudden jolt woke me with a gasp. I was on the bus to

Clearmont, passengers shrieking in the dark as it fishtailed on the snowy road. The driver yelled, "Hold on!" An overhead bin sprung open and something hit the floor with a heavy thump. A child screamed, and I grabbed the seat ahead of me, clenching my teeth anticipating impact. Instead, we slid to a stop, the abrupt silence broken by a baby's cry.

The driver turned, grabbing the support pole behind him. He pulled to his feet. "Everybody okay?"

Through several murmurs of assent, more children began to sob.

A man in front of me stretched his neck to look above the seat ahead of him. "What happened?"

The driver glanced toward the windshield. "Sorry about the sudden stop, folks. Someone who passed us a mile or so back, has stopped in the middle of the road. If you'll all stay calm, I'm going to go see what's up."

Blowing snow swirled inside as the driver left the bus, and someone nearby closed the door behind him. Others stood in the aisle trying to see out the windshield. Mothers comforted children, and many turned on their small cabin lights while we waited for the driver's return.

I put my head down and pressed fingers to my forehead, wincing from a sudden headache.

A minute passed while people gathered scattered belongings and settled down to wait. Then harsh pounding on the bus door startled everyone anew. The door opened, and I lifted my head.

Climbing the steps ahead of the driver, Brock appeared,

scanning the cabin. I slid down in my seat, but not before his eyes locked on mine.

Without missing a beat, Brock's countenance shifted to beaming adoration. "Darling!" he exclaimed. What was he up to? It reminded me of one evening at Christmas when he picked me up for a fancy dinner date. I had considered his manner a bit exaggerated, but sweet back then. Now it frightened me.

He came down the aisle, his head tilted in a show of loving concern. "You don't know how worried I've been, but don't fret about it, honey. Everything's fine now." He reached down and took hold of my elbow.

"Why can't you just leave me alone?" I kept my voice low while resisting the tug on my arm. "I already told you it's over between us. I want to go on by myself."

"But darling, there's no need to worry." His voice was acid-laced honey with determined eyes registering behind his beaming countenance.

His grip tightened and he pulled me to stand. His eyes remained constant, his voice resonating with devoted care. "I'm going to take care of everything—you and the baby. I need you to come home, honey."

He had drawn me close, so I held my voice to a whisper. "What's wrong with you?"

Brock ignored me. "C'mon, babe. Let me take you home. I know we can patch things up."

Someone nearby got caught up in Brock's emotional appeal. "Give him a chance."

I glanced around me. A tide of sympathy had swelled toward Brock, the poor scorned sweetheart. Or husband.

Or whatever he was trying to be. His grip on my elbow was firm as he maneuvered me toward the front of the bus.

The time for subtlety had passed. "Stop." I protested loudly through gritted teeth.

He wrapped his free arm around my shoulder and pressed me forward. We reached the driver, who stood beside his seat, his sympathetic eyes focused on Brock.

I leaned into the driver's line of vision. "It's not true, you know. I'm not even pregnant. This is just a costume."

He didn't answer me, but looked to Brock, his brow pinched with concern. "I'm glad you were able to track her down. Do you think she'll be all right?"

"The doctors said she might have times of confusion. I'll make sure she gets the right help."

The driver opened the door and, a moment later, I was out in the blowing snow. "I don't even have my coat, Brock. Do you want me to freeze?"

He pulled me a few feet from the door and let go of my elbow with a shove. "It wasn't your coat any more than the rest of this get-up. Just get in the car. The heater's on."

I glanced at the car, sitting sideways on the road in the halo of bus headlights and took a slow backward step. "Why are you doing this? Why can't you leave me alone?"

His brows slanted. "Don't make a scene, Penny. They already think you're acting crazy."

"*I'm* acting crazy?" A tear dropped to my cheek, stinging in the icy wind. "Look at us. We're standing out in a blizzard because you can't bear to let me go."

"You have to come with me, Penny."

"No I don't." I took a couple more steps back.

"I'm not asking. I'm telling you." He pulled his hand up slowly from his coat pocket, revealing a small handgun. He kept it close to his waist, but it was pointed right at me.

"What?" My breath expelled with that one word, and my vision narrowed to a tunnel.

Would I ever breathe again?

TWENTY

Lance stared at the waiting room clock, forearms braced against jittery knees. The tick of the second hand had become the meter of his thoughts mentally reciting the litany of steps required to complete Penny's craniotomy.

Pastor Mark, sitting in an adjacent seat, read his Bible. They had prayed and paced the floor for hours. Friends and church family had been contacted, many of whom shared encouragements based on their own experiences with difficult circumstances. He knew the chain of prayer would extend quickly through social media, texts, and calls, raising a chorus of continuing intercession as the clock hands crept toward midday.

Waiting outside the surgical bay hadn't been Lance's idea, but Dr. Matheson had insisted upon it in gentle but unyielding tones. Instead, Lance focused on turning over his stresses to the Lord in order to endure this unfamiliar territory of waiting and uncertainty. Dr. Matheson's assuring words had reminded him of his wife's when she decided to end further cancer treatments. "Don't worry. I know what I'm doing," Marla had said, her eyes reflecting like deep watery pools. "This is not the end. It will be okay."

He blinked at the memory and pulled back his frayed emotions to focus on visualizing Penny's procedure. She had to survive this. He couldn't face the idea of losing her too.

The clock's tempo resumed as he mentally reviewed each step required for the surgery and imagined each tool slapped into the surgeon's hand. If only her life weren't dependent on the precision of others.

Thoughts of Brock also intruded his thoughts. Penny's boyfriend had disappeared with the arrival of the crash cart team, yet he remained a concern. It was highly unlikely the young man's presence had triggered the seizure, but the episode seemed to have spooked him off, and as far as Lance was concerned, that was for the best.

Nagging holes in Brock's story plagued his thoughts. Lance had discussed them with Mark, but neither of them knew what next step to pursue. With any luck, the guy was on his way back to Phoenix and would remain out of the picture.

Lance stood and stretched his shoulders.

Mark closed his Bible and looked up. "Do you want me to go find us a couple burgers or something?"

"Nah." Lance rotated his neck and shook the tension from his arms. "I'm not really hungry. But you could go if you want."

"It's no trouble, and you might be hungry later. We could nuke it." His brows lifted. "Or I could just pick up some pastries from the donut shop across the street."

Lance gave him a sideways glance and smirked. "Frankly, Mark, sometimes your diet choices scare me."

"Yeah, Jackie says the same thing."

Lance blew out his nervousness with a chuckle. "Get whatever lunch you want for yourself. Hopefully, by the time you get back we'll have some news on the surgery."

"I'm okay with sticking around until then. We can eat later, after things are more settled."

The elevator door chimed, and they both looked across the hall. It opened and Sergeant Clemens stepped out, accompanied by a young woman with spiked yellow hair. This, along with her bright geometric-print yoga pants and pensive expression made it clear she wasn't another officer.

They approached, and Clemens acknowledged Mark with a brief nod before turning his attention to Lance. "Dr. Doyle. I'm glad I found you here. If you have some time, I have some new case developments that I'd like to discuss with you."

"Certainly." Lance gestured toward Mark. "You haven't met my pastor yet. This is Mark Lindmeyer." They shook hands. "Mark, this is Sergeant Clemens, who has been following up on leads for the missing person's case at Penny's college. In the process, he helped locate Penny." Lance took a breath. "Unfortunately, my daughter suffered a stroke this morning and we've been waiting for her surgery results. I sure hope you have some good news." He nodded to the girl. "I see you brought someone with you."

Clemens cleared his throat. "Yes. This is Hope

McAllister. She spent several hours with your daughter just before the bus left the station in Barrett. She wanted to add her support."

The girl stepped forward and shook Lance's hand. Beyond her rather extreme makeup choice Lance saw kindness in her eyes.

"Mr. Doyle," she said with a soft voice. "I had no idea Penny had been injured. I heard about the bus crash, of course, but her name wasn't on the injured list, so I assumed she was one of the lucky ones. Had I known, I would have come right away."

Me too, Lance thought to himself. "Thank you. I'm curious though, how do you know my daughter?"

She glanced briefly at the floor. "We met on Saturday so I don't know her well, but I tried to help when things went wrong between her and Brock."

Lance's interest piqued. *So, their relationship had derailed.* "I'd appreciate it if you could share what happened in detail."

Hope nodded. "Sure. I already told Sergeant Clemens, but when Penny and her boyfriend came into the café where I work, she was upset. I guess she wanted to break it off with him, but didn't know how to tell him. She wrote him a note on a napkin when he was away from the table and then asked me to help her sneak out of the café. He stayed around town all day looking for her, so later in the evening, I helped her sneak onto the bus."

"So, you've met Brock?"

She twisted her mouth to one side. "Well, we weren't introduced. I just took their lunch order and then caught an earful from him after Penny left the café. He's a pretty intense guy."

This put a new twist on things. Lance rubbed the back of his neck, frustration welling. He looked over to Pastor Mark, who'd been listening with wide eyes. "She broke up with him. I knew he was trying to hide something." Turning back to Hope and Sergeant Clemens, he added, "That guy hasn't been upfront with me since I met him. That put my radar up right away."

Clemens interjected, "Are you talking about the guy we saw here in the waiting room yesterday?"

"Yeah. I talked to him for a while after you left. He wanted to see Penny and I put him off until this morning."

Hope's mouth dropped open. She touched Lance's forearm. "He's here? Penny was scared of him. I don't know everything that happened between them, but I wondered if he was one of those stalker-types."

Lance bit his lip. Maybe that's why he had been parked at the house. "What makes you think he's a stalker?"

Hope's brow remained furrowed. "It's like he can't accept that she left him. He went all over town looking for her and waited at the bus station that evening too." Hope pulled out her phone. "In fact, I got a call shortly after the bus left and I'm sure it's him. I didn't recognize the number, so I recorded it." She punched a button, starting the playback.

"Hope?" The man's voice was accompanied by wind noise.

"Yes? Who is this?"

"Are you … on the bus?" The words were measured out, with a tone of underlying accusation.

A long silence followed, indicating Hope's heightened awareness. Or fear.

He spoke again, in a voice that carried the edge of a knife. "Yeah, I wondered about that. You think you're *so* smart, but you can't fool me." The recording ended.

"That's when I hung up and blocked his number." Hope looked up from the phone. "It's gotta be him. There's no one else it could be."

Lance exhaled. "Why didn't you call the cops?"

Hope's eyes dropped. "I don't know. I guess it didn't seem like something they could do anything about. The next day, when I heard about the crash and how the driver was killed, I felt sick all over again, but by that time the investigators were already involved with the whole thing and so I … I don't know." Her voice cracked and she started to cry. "I wanted to believe it was over … and I thought Penny wasn't injured—"

Clemens interjected, "But there were reports about an unidentified female."

Hope's mascara pooled below her eyes. "I never heard that. I thought she was okay..." She turned to Lance as black streaks ran to her chin and dripped to the front of her blouse. "I thought she got back home to you. That's all she wanted to do."

Lance offered his handkerchief. "Well, let's not dwell on that now. I'm more concerned about what Brock's up to." He shook his head. "And to think I let him spend time with her this morning."

Hope looked to Sergeant Clemens, her face still etched with concern. "Is there anything you can do? Take him into custody or something?"

Clemens shook his head. "There's no reason to detain him—at least not yet." He swiveled toward Lance. "I'd sure like to speak with him, though."

Lance shrugged. "He left when Penny had the stroke. I don't know where he is now, but his SUV is gone from the parking lot."

Clemens' forehead creased. "What kind of SUV?"

"A Toyota Highlander. Dark gray. Why?"

Clemens scrubbed his chin. "I was talking with the crash investigators yesterday. They're looking for a late model Highlander in connection with the bus crash."

Lance looked aside, visualizing the SUV. "I didn't notice any damage on his vehicle."

"We don't think they collided. Some of the passengers mentioned an aggressive driver with a dark vehicle on the road that night. Their reports along with tire impressions at the scene indicate the Highlander was in the left lane and stopped for a time at the crash site. It's still undetermined whether it forced the bus off the road or just stopped after encountering the crash and then left the scene."

Leaving the scene of a bus crash? Who would do such a thing? Brock was no prize, but this seemed over the top. A lead weight bore down on Lance's shoulders. His knees weakened.

Clemens put his hand out toward the waiting room

chairs. "Have a seat, doctor. I'm afraid there's more you need to hear."

More? Lance walked toward a chair, but turned without sitting. "More news about the crash or about Penny's connection to the murdered girl?"

"About the murder."

Lance didn't like the somber tone of Clemens' voice. Before he could reply, the elevator chimed, drawing everyone's attention. The doors opened and Dr. Matheson stepped out. Lance moved forward as she surveyed the group surrounding him. His pulse quickened. "How's Penny doing?"

"Your daughter's a fortunate young woman." She glanced again to the group, "She's not out of the woods yet, but she apparently has more fight in her than I gave her credit for."

Weight lifted from Lance's shoulders. He nodded, thinking of his wife's courageous battle against cancer. "Yeah. She got that from her mother."

TWENTY-ONE

Were my eyes deceiving me or had Brock gone mad? I stood only a few feet away, so there was no mistaking the gun muzzle pointed directly at my gut. I blinked and forced myself to breathe. Would he actually shoot me? A glance into his piercing dark eyes told me he was deadly serious.

"What's going on, Brock?" I winced against the sting of icy snowflakes blowing into my face. "Why can't you just let me go?"

Brock snarled his answer. "You know."

"Know what?" The black look on his face made my heart pound. "What arc you talking about?"

"You've been trying to hide it, but *we* know better."

Brock's words made no sense. I extended both arms and shrugged my shoulders. "Who's we?" Tremors shook from my fingers, so I quickly clasped my arms back around my torso. "And what do you think I'm hiding?"

"You fought like crazy that night. Screamed and clawed. You shouldn't have even had the strength to fight. That means the G-Juice didn't work, and if it didn't work, your memory is fine." He shook his head, and I heard a metallic click. He had cocked the gun, preparing to fire. "I wanted to believe you, but Tyler's right. You're just too big of a risk—especially with the NFL draft just around the corner. There's too much at stake."

"Brock, I don't know what you're talking about." My voice faltered because, in a strange way, his statement had started to make a little bit of sense. He had insisted I was drunk at the party, but now I wondered if he had expected or planned that I would be drunk enough on whatever G-Juice was to forget New Year's Eve.

A creaking sound from the bus caused Brock's expression to change abruptly. He withdrew the gun, shifting it behind his back, and took a deep breath, his lips taut.

Turning, I saw the bus driver step down, his boots crunching on the packed snow. He held out the coat I had stored in the overhead bin. "Miss, I think you forgot something."

"Oh yes." The words tumbled out as I rushed to him. I took hold of the coat and quickly stepped up through the open door. "Thank you so much."

At the top step, I turned. The driver looked from me to Brock and back again. "But I thought you were…"

"No, I'm staying on the bus. Sorry for the inconvenience." My eyes lifted to the place where Brock still stood out in front of the bus, but with the cab lights on, I couldn't see him. Only blowing snow that swirled against the dark windshield. Would he be rash enough to fire at me through it? I didn't want to find out. I headed down the aisle, while the passengers eyed me with wary faces. Someone hushed a child. Another shook their head in disapproval as I maneuvered to my seat. Sitting, I slouched low and spread the coat over my lap. Ducking my head, I avoided their stares.

The driver reentered and stood at the head of the aisle. "Are you sure you know what you're doing, miss? That fellow out there seems quite determined to win you back."

"Positive. I paid for my ticket. I want to stay on this bus." *Please, let's leave. Now.*

He scratched his head, then headed back outside. My heart sank. If he let Brock back onto the bus, I'd be doomed. My only hope was if the driver would talk some sense into him. Convince him to give up and go home.

Then a new thought made my heart skip. Was Brock crazy enough to shoot the driver?

"Hey," someone called out. "Are we gonna move or what?"

Another guy near the front replied. "I think he's telling her husband to move his vehicle."

If only Brock would leave me alone. The thought of him harming others made me burrow deeper under my coat. Perhaps I should have warned the driver about the gun. Things had gone so crazy; it seemed anything could happen. I chewed on my thumbnail and discovered my hands were trembling.

Moments passed, while I wondered if Brock would return to drag me back out the door. Finally, throwing off the coat, I pulled myself up to stand with the pillow still awkwardly strapped to my stomach. Making my way back to the bathroom, I locked myself in—again.

From the relative safety of this make-shift cocoon, I stared into the mirror over the sink. No prying eyes here. Only my own, haggard as they were. I pulled off the wig and dropped it on the floor. My hair was a flattened mess, but how could that matter? The masquerade was over.

"Please go away. Please go away." I whispered a plea to the deaf walls.

Waiting in the silence was interminable, but hearing gunshots would have been worse.

With the help of soap and water and several tissues, I began to clean Hope's makeup from my face while trying to calm my jitters. "God. Oh, God. Please help me. Make him go away."

Then abruptly, the bus engine engaged and we were moving again. I raised my head from the sink, and a flood of relief and gratitude made my knees weak. I leaned against the counter as tears surfaced.

"God, please, what has happened to me? I just want to feel safe again." I dropped to my knees in the cramped space and cried until I'd drawn the last tissue from the dispenser. "I need your help, God. Please."

The bus engine rumbled over the sounds of my weeping and, at last, my tears were spent. I blew my nose one last time, picked myself up and began peeling away the layers of Hope's costume. I unstrapped the pillow and redressed as best I could from the cast-offs. I finger-combed my hair and splashed cool water on my face.

A final look in the mirror revealed puffy bare skin with reddened eyes and nose. This was me: raw and empty. A broken mess. What would Dad think of me now?

I pushed aside the old recurring worry. More than ever, I wanted—no, I needed—to get home.

Slowly, I slid open the bathroom door and peeked out. I expected all heads to turn, judgment written on their faces, but no one was watching. In fact, everyone but the driver appeared to be asleep.

I maneuvered past the rows of passengers, some with limbs hanging in the aisle or slumped with their heads bobbing on their chests. Then, as I approached my row, I saw the top of someone's head in the seat next to mine.

Someone with curly white hair.

There, sitting in the window seat as I stepped up next to her, was Mrs. Wilton, with crochet hook and thread in hand. She looked over her wire-glasses with a smile. "Oh, there you are. I was beginning to wonder—you were in there so long."

TWENTY-TWO

Lance perched on the edge of an armchair, while Sergeant Clemens scanned a sheaf of paperwork on his clipboard. Dr. Matheson had shown them to a small consultation room before returning to her patients. The space might have been originally designed as a janitorial closet. It had just enough room for two cushioned chairs and a side table with a lamp. A framed seaside print by Monet hung on the wall, apparently to lend the space some warmth or a calming effect, though Lance felt neither. Not while his daughter lay in the recovery room with a hole surgically bored through her skull.

"Here it is." Clemens pulled one sheet out from the rest. "The autopsy on the Maxwell girl came back indicating the presence of alcohol and GHB in her system. Both were probably ingested during the New Year's Eve party." With scrunched brows and tilted head, he read through a pair of slender reading glasses. "Cause of death was 'hypoxia, via respiratory depression.' I'm told that means she OD'd on the stuff and stopped breathing."

Lance shifted in his seat. "Yeah. It's easy to overdose that stuff, especially if you're mixing it with alcohol." He shook his head. "I can't even imagine Penny attending a party with drugs and alcohol."

"I hear that sort of thing from parents all the time." Clemens removed his glasses and looked directly at Lance. "I'm told that two people at this party described a fight between Penny and Miss Maxwell that evening."

Could it be true? Lance remembered the older injuries he'd seen listed on Penny's intake form. "I suppose that's possible, but does it matter? You said the girl didn't die as a result of a fight."

"Correct. It doesn't explain how her body ended up out in the woods either. What the fight does suggest is a possible motive for the overdose."

"You're saying the overdose wasn't accidental?"

Clemens tapped the glasses on the paperwork in his hand. "That's one of the things Maricopa County has been trying to figure out."

"Did these witnesses say why Penny fought with her?"

Clemens tucked the autopsy sheet away. "Apparently both girls were drunk at the time. Jealousy has been suggested."

Penny had never been the jealous type, but then, she'd never been a drinker either. Lance shook his head again. "Penny always got along with people. She had lots of friends growing up."

Clemens folded the glasses and tucked them in his pocket. "Lots of things happen to kids away at college that would never happen at home."

"You have any kids?"

"I have a daughter in Montrose, married with two kids

of her own nearly half-grown. I'll admit, it's a different world now than the one she grew up in."

It was hard to argue with that. Lance leaned forward in the chair, preparing to stand. "So, is there anything else I need to know?"

"Yeah. About the two witnesses to this fight. One is the murdered girl's boyfriend. Personally, I think there's reason to believe he might have a bigger role in this."

"But Maricopa isn't considering him?"

"Not as long as his story holds up. He says the party broke up early, and that's when the girls had their tiff. He and his buddy broke up the fight and the buddy took both girls back to the campus dorms."

"Then maybe his buddy is involved."

"That's also possible."

"So, what's being done about him?"

"They've been looking for him for a few days now. It turns out he left campus shortly after he was first questioned."

Lance stood up and raked his hands through his hair. "This is frustrating. Don't they have any leads on where he may have gone?"

"They didn't, at least not until I went to Barrett and spoke with Hope. She informed me that he's in this area, and you've just confirmed that he's been here at the hospital."

Lance spun to face him. "He's here?"

"Yeah. He's Penny's boyfriend, Brock Harper."

More pieces began to mentally slide into place. Lance straightened his spine and took a deep breath as new concerns overcame his initial surprise. "So it appears my issues with Brock are compounding. I should have guessed."

Clemens tapped his papers together and clipped them. "I will need to talk with him if he shows up again."

"Can we put hospital security on alert to watch for him?"

The officer stood. "Good idea. I'll have a chat with them on my way out."

"He might be gone for good, though, especially if he thinks you're catching up with him."

Clemens patted Lance on the shoulder. "Don't worry. I don't expect he'll get too far."

TWENTY-THREE

The impossibility of Mrs. Wilton's appearance on the bus confounded me, yet, there she sat with her crocheting in hand and eyes crinkled with good cheer. "You know," she said matter-of-factly, "It never ceases to amaze me how many people choose bathrooms as a place to call out to the Almighty."

"Mrs. Wilton, how did you get here?" I dropped into the seat next to her and interrupted her handiwork by wrapping my hands around hers.

She returned my astonished gaze. "You did call upon the Lord for help, did you not? Don't be surprised He has answered you, Penny. I'm here at His bidding."

What was she saying? I pulled back, hesitant to ask. "Are you implying that you are some kind of an angel?"

She glanced up briefly in thought. "Some kind? I suppose so, but only the most common variety."

I shook my head. What could be common about the appearance of *any* kind of angel? "So, you don't own that old inn in Dalton?"

"I never said I did." She seemed surprised I would make that assumption.

I giggled, in spite of my astonishment. "That's right. You didn't."

"Well, you've been through quite a scare and I suppose that, along with everything else, has led you to this moment."

"Do you know what happened at the New Year's Eve party? And about Brock? Did you know he has a gun? I think he and Tyler want me dead."

"No, dear. I'm not privy to the details of all these things. But I know the One Who is."

"You mean God."

She nodded.

"Frankly, Mrs. Wilton, if He knew these things, why didn't He help me back then."

"Because He's helping you now, dear."

Her logic was too simplistic. I pulled back in frustration. "But if He'd helped me back then, I might not be here right now."

She smiled. "Precisely. My guess is He knew *this* was the place you needed to be."

"But that doesn't make any sense."

"It may not make sense right now, but it will." Her gray eyes exuded unwavering confidence.

"But you don't know what I've been through."

"You could tell me about it."

I took a breath and shook my head. "I don't even remember parts of it."

"Try. Start with the things you do remember."

What could I tell this kindly old woman—or angel—

who probably knew nothing about parties with drinking and dancing? I squirmed inwardly, feeling awkward, but if Mrs. Wilton sensed anything amiss, she didn't show it. She set her crocheting aside and waited patiently with a tender expression.

The dream from which I'd just awakened was fresh in my mind, so I started there, telling about Abbi's seductive dance and the other partiers who left early. I talked about feeling woozy as I stood up from the sofa. "…and after I lost my balance, I woke up here on the bus."

She listened patiently. "But while you were at the party, what happened after you got woozy?"

"I don't know. It's one of the gaps, I guess." I looked down, fiddling with my hands in my lap.

Mrs. Wilton gently laid her gnarled fingers on top of mine. "Do you have any other memories from the party?" she asked softly.

"Not much, really. At some point, I noticed Abbi had passed out."

"Where was she?"

"In the living room, collapsed across one of the arm chairs. It's hardly more than a snapshot in my mind. I don't remember what led up to it or what happened after."

"Why do you think these memories elude you?"

"Maybe… I was passed out too?"

"But you said you weren't drunk like everyone else."

"That's right." What was it Brock had said outside the bus? Something about a juice that hadn't worked. "Maybe I was drugged."

Mrs. Wilton shook her head. "Oh, how easily mankind succumbs to Lucifer's snares." She leaned forward, catching my downcast eyes. "But the good news is, you weren't drugged 'enough.' Your memories remain—they've only been in hiding, waiting for the right time."

"And when will that be?"

"When you are ready to trust Him with them."

"That just doesn't make sense, Mrs. Wilton. It's not like memories have some kind of willpower. How can they decide to stay hidden?"

"It's not the memories that have willpower. It's you." Her steady eyes pierced through me.

"But I've been trying to remember all along."

"Give them to Jesus."

Jesus. How could I give anything to Him after He let Mom die? Tears sprang again to my eyes, burning hot as they spilled down my cheeks. "I... I..."

Mrs. Wilton shifted in her seat to extend an arm over my shoulder. Her other hand laid a hanky on my lap. "There, there, child. Dry your tears. The Lord knows your doubts. He would have you draw near with a sincere heart and the full assurance that faith brings."

"But I don't have faith—not in God."

"So, who else would you trust?"

Who else? I dabbed at my nose with the hanky. "You?"

"Me?" She pulled back, clutching the collar of her housedress. "Don't trust only with your eyes, Penny."

"I... I'm trying." Warmth flowed through me. Was Jesus nearby?

She placed her hand atop my head and began to pray softly. In moments, my eyes grew too heavy to stay open.

***

I was back at Tyler's house on New Year's Eve.

"This way." Brock steered me down the hall with his arm around my waist. My head hung down, bobbing against my chest while he half-carried me. Through the circle of hair that hung around my face, I noticed my shoes were gone though I couldn't recall removing them.

Dim light filtered past us from behind. Then he turned through a dark doorway and dumped me, face-down on a bed. The door closed. I rolled my head to the side and pulled my hand up under my shoulder. *Push. Get up.* But I only managed to shift my elbow.

Brief flashes of light illuminated the window shade, accompanied by crackling explosions. Fireworks.

I could hear Brock rummaging in a drawer somewhere behind me.

"Help me." I managed the words, though my tongue felt thick.

"Patience, babe." Brock chuckled, as if making an inside joke. "We don't want to hurry this, do we?"

He reached for my shoulder and rolled me toward him, then drew back the hair that splayed across my face. Cupping my chin in his hand, he leaned close. "That better?" His breath smelled of liquor.

"What's wrong with me?" My teeth began to chatter, though the room was warm.

"Nothing I can't help you fix." He smiled, his eyes lecherously wicked as he began to unbutton my blouse.

"What?" I managed to lift my hands, but they flailed uselessly against his. "Stop."

He put his mouth against mine, closing off my protest as his hands continued tugging at my clothes.

A fist pounded twice on the door.

"Not now!" Brock pulled away, his voice harsh.

The door flew open. "Come here, man." Tyler's voice emanated panic. He didn't wait for Brock, but ran back down the hall.

Brock cocked an eyebrow, unfazed by Tyler's anxiety. He leaned toward me again. "Don't go anywhere." He left the room with a chuckle.

With several deep breaths of effort, I rolled toward the edge of the bed, my head swimming. My hands tingled as I worked to sit upright and the effort brought a wave of choking nausea. Leaning over my knees, I spat bile onto the rug and nearly toppled to the floor.

What was wrong with me? Lifting my head brought on a sudden ache that bored into my left temple. I reached up, and felt the pain pulse and swell. Squinting with a cry, I flopped on my side at the edge of the bed, curling against the pain. Who could help me? Who could even hear? No one. No one but… I breathed a whimper, "Jesus."

My mind drifted to black under heavy eyelids.

An unfamiliar sound, something dragging or scraping, caused me to open my eyes some time later. Had I been asleep? Unconscious? How long? The light level was the same as before, suggesting little time had passed. The fireworks, however, had ceased. Again, the sound, like rough fabric scraping, came from another room down the hall. Sounds of something heavy being shifted. Like furniture on a gritty floor. Hesitantly, I pulled myself up to sit on the edge of the bed again. My limbs seemed a bit more cooperative, though my head still felt heavy and dull, and I shivered from a sweat-induced chill.

I sucked in my breath at the sound of a door opening, but it was elsewhere in the house. The front door perhaps? No. I didn't hear the storm door. Maybe a back door then? More scraping noises and then the same door closed.

Had Brock left?

I attempted standing. It required all the effort I could muster. My legs were rubbery and my feet felt like stones. Once upright, I sagged against the wall, but managed to keep my knees from buckling. With clumsy hands, I pulled my blouse together attempting a partially-effective tuck into the waistband of my skirt. I drug one foot toward the open doorway and slid along the wall. Again, the headache swelled near my left-temple and drilled into the core of my brain. I stopped to reach up, as if pressure might keep it from exploding. With effort, I managed another dragging step.

Fumbling to grasp the doorframe with clumsy fingers, I peeked into the hall. A narrow sliver of light from the kitchen was visible at the end of the hall. The rest of the house was dark.

Then the distant door opened again and I drew back as voices broke the silence.

"There is no time for that now." Brock's voice had a sharp edge.

"We can't just leave her here." Tyler spat the words with a low voice. "It has to be tonight. There's no other way."

"We'll deal with it tomorrow after the workout, but right now, I've gotta get Penny back to the dorms while she's still under."

"This is messed up, man. If anyone finds out—"

"Ty, get a grip. No one will find out."

Brock's footsteps crossed the kitchen tile and my heart skipped in panic. He was coming to get me. I swallowed and turned back toward the bed, causing my brain to spin. My feet drug as if through deep water. What would he do if he saw I was awake? I reached for the edge of the bed and stumbled, falling in a heap on the floor.

Brock reached the doorway a moment later. I closed my eyes, wondering what he thought of me lying crumpled on the carpet.

He rushed over and bent to lift me. "Fell out of bed? Looks like our party ends early tonight, babe." He turned my face toward him, stroking my cheek with his finger. "A pity, I know. Maybe another time."

I feigned unconsciousness as he pulled me upright. Would he notice the shirttails I'd tucked in? Then he'd know I was awake. I didn't risk opening my eyes.

Brock pulled me down the hall as before, my head lolling against my chest. I watched the floor as we passed through the living room and kitchen. It sparkled with bits of glitter. At the back door, he wrapped an arm around my chest in order to back up and turn the knob behind him with his free hand.

It creaked open and he pulled me through to a wooden platform in the garage. The lights were on and I sensed the exterior overhead door was closed. No chance of running out into the night, even if my body would have cooperated with such an effort. I only hoped he would take me back to the dorm, as he'd said.

The garage level was a few steps lower than the main level of the house. Wooden stairs followed along the back wall from the platform.

"What are you doing?" Brock asked as he shifted me around in order to start backing down the stairs. He sounded annoyed. Panic seized me until I realized he was talking to Tyler, who was crouched on the floor below the platform holding the edge of a blue plastic tarp. On the floor at his knee, Abbi Maxwell lay with open, expressionless eyes and her complexion grey in the dim light.

Tyler shifted his gaze upward at Brock's question. His eyes locked with mine. Shock registered and his brows raised. He tossed the tarp over Abbi's still form. "She's awake," he yelled. "I thought you said she was out cold."

Brock grunted in surprise, and cinched his arm against my chest with crushing force. Then he released and shoved me away with his free hand against my back.

I was flung to the railing, and lurched over it, bending at the waist while my arms hung useless, as if reaching for the tarp that covered Abbi below me. I flailed against the balusters while my feet scraped the platform, unable to gain a foothold.

Then I saw Abbi's feet extending from the far end of the tarp, and a strong sense of premonition washed over me. I'd seen this before.

Bare feet on concrete.

TWENTY-FOUR

L ance leaned against the doorframe, arms crossed, and watched Hope, who sat beside Penny's bed patting her hand and chatting in soft tones. Though Penny remained unresponsive, her vitals had stayed stable since the surgery. Most inexplicable was her recent neurology report, which continued to show high activity in the memory centers of her brain.

"You breezed right through your surgery," Hope said. "Soon you'll be waking up and I know everything's going to be just fine."

Though Lance might not have characterized Penny's surgery as a "breeze," Hope's soothing tone made him smile.

They had talked while Penny was still in the surgical recovery room. Hope described the details of Penny's costumed escape, and it gave him a greater appreciation for his daughter's quirky new friend. She had been a real blessing when Penny needed it most.

He wasn't aware whether Penny had any close friends at school. It bothered him to know so little of her life at college. Though she had been the one to pull away, he'd also been at fault. So lost in grief after Marla's passing that he had let his only child slip farther and farther away.

They'd both lost too much. He prayed he'd get another chance once Penny recovered and all the mess with the murdered girl was sorted out.

He pulled away from the doorframe to straighten his back. "I have a question for you, Hope."

"Yes?" She twisted to peer over her shoulder with her arm on the back of the chair.

"Maybe Sergeant Clemens already talked to you about this, but did Penny say anything to you about a missing girl at her college?"

"Oh yeah." She pursed her lips, thinking. "She said some investigators wanted to talk with her, but she didn't have any information to give them."

"Did she mention anything about an altercation with this girl on the night of the New Year's Eve party?"

Hope's brows rose. "She did. She said Brock had accused her of being in a fight. He implied that it had something to do with the girl's disappearance." She drummed her fingers a couple times on the chair back. "I'm pretty sure that was the final straw—the reason Penny broke it off with him."

"So, she *didn't* fight with the girl?"

"No. She was really emphatic about that."

"Did you tell Sergeant Clemens this?"

"I did, and I think he's talked with the investigators in Arizona about it too."

Relieved, Lance nodded. "That's good to know. Did Penny say anything else?"

"Not really. We were mainly focused on getting her disguise together." Hope turned back and patted Penny's hand. "I know it's been a bumpy road, but the doctors say you're progressing really well. When you wake up, I think everything's going to come together for you. I probably won't even have to bring you any pie."

Pie? Lance tilted his head, wondering at the comment, but footsteps approaching in the hallway caught his attention. He leaned out the door and saw Dr. Matheson march toward him, her open lab coat revealing a two-toned light blue dress that perfectly suited her complexion.

She held up her tablet with a smile and called out, "It's all good news, Doctor Doyle."

He backed out the door to face her. "Please, I wish you would call me Lance."

She stopped in front of him. "All right. And you can call me Amelia."

Amelia. With her accent, it sounded almost musical.

She raised her brows. "So, are you interested in the newest MRI results?"

Lance blinked. "Huh? Oh yes, of course."

She tapped the screen and pointed to a series of brain scans. "You already know the intracranial pressure is holding steady within a normal range and these scans show the affected area is already responding to the reduced pressure. There are no signs of axonal injury or other complications. She was fortunate to be here to get immediate attention when the aneurysm ruptured."

"Oh, I wouldn't call it fortunate, Doctor. I mean, Amelia."

"Oh?"

"No, I think God has a way of putting us right where we need to be, right when we need to be there." He stole another look into her eyes. "And He places the right people in our path when we need them too."

She smiled and held his gaze. "Well, Lance, I didn't realize you were so spiritually-tuned, but I do heartily agree."

Lance smiled as she passed him through the doorway and approached Penny's bedside. He followed, standing behind Hope's chair while Amelia gently lifted one of Penny's eyelids and flicked a small light across her eyes. Then she listened briefly to her heart and lungs with a stethoscope.

She leaned down, placing her hand gently against Penny's bruised cheek. "Penny? Can you hear me? This is Doctor Matheson. You had a little excitement earlier today, but everything is under control now. Keep up the good work of healing and resting. You have people looking forward to seeing you well again."

Lance smiled at Amelia's gentle care for his daughter.

After she left to continue her rounds, Hope got up from her chair beside Penny's bed. "You seem very tired, Mr. Doyle. Could I get you something? Coffee, maybe?"

"You're right. I *am* tired. I haven't been home since yesterday and didn't have a chance to bring a change of clothes."

"Why don't you let me watch over Penny while you drive home and get the things you need? I'll be heading back to Barrett later tonight, but I can stick around until you get back and I'll call you if anything comes up while you're gone."

Though he felt reluctant, it made sense. "Yeah, that's a good idea."

They exchanged phone numbers and shortly after, Lance was in his car, headed down the pass toward Clearmont under a blue sky.

An hour later, as he pulled into his driveway, Brock came to mind again but there was no sign of him or his vehicle. Relieved, Lance carried mail in from the box and laid it on the counter. He stood in the kitchen, silence enveloping him as it had so many other days since Penny left.

Hominess was reserved for places where life happened. This house was a place where time had stood still for the past four years. So many untouched rooms, existing only as places where Marla's sense of décor and orderliness kept her memory close. If he and Penny were going to have a chance to patch the brokenness in their relationship, things around the house would have to change.

He found a backpack in a closet and began to load it with toiletries and clothes. Penny could waken at any time. He would ask Amelia about a transfer to Mercy Medical as soon as possible after that. It would be helpful to have her close to home during the remaining weeks of her recovery.

And once she was home… He bit his lip and dared to project his hopes toward the future. Once home, Penny would need to take time off from school for physical therapy and other transitional support. It would be a chance for him to work on mending their relationship. As she grew stronger, perhaps they'd find ways to spruce up the house. Rearrange the furniture or repaint. Anything that would help rebuild their family bond. Anything to keep her at home for a little while longer.

Would Penny even consider such a thing? He allowed himself to entertain the thought as he took a quick shower, finished packing his overnight bag and began the long drive back up the canyon.

TWENTY-FIVE

The sight of Abbi Maxwell's feet extending out from under the tarp covering her still body hit me like a jolt of lightning—singeing itself into the core of my being and setting many other disturbing memories in sharp relief. It explained the dizzy tunnel vision I'd experienced upon seeing the garage mechanic's feet sticking out from under the car in Dalton. The lecherous look of the station attendant on the previous night also came to mind because it matched the look in Brock's eyes when he hovered over me on New Year's Eve.

Mrs. Wilton was right. The memories had always been there. I had just closed my mind, unwilling to revisit them.

Until now. Finally, I was ready to face what I'd witnessed, and when I did, I opened my eyes and found I had laid my head in Mrs. Wilton's lap holding her hanky to my face. With a sigh, I sat up and dabbed my eyes.

Mrs. Wilton tucked a stray strand of hair behind my ear. "I'm sorry for all you've been through, Penny. Do you remember New Year's Eve now?

I nodded. "Enough of it. You were right. I've always known what happened."

She tilted her head. "So, tell me dear. What frightened you so much that you needed to lock those memories away?"

More images flooded through the broken wall in my mind. Flashes of staggered moves and swirling dizziness, as I fought for my life. But it wasn't a fight against Abbi. No. I had fought with Brock while on the stair landing in the garage.

"Oftentimes healing comes with the telling." Mrs. Wilton said, her voice like a soothing balm.

"I was so afraid. Abbi was dead and I … I knew I would be next. I tried to fight … to yell. Anything to get away." I blew my nose in her hanky. "I tried my best, but my hands … my feet … they were nearly useless. Brock grabbed me by my shoulder and jerked me around while I struggled to get away from him. And the look on his face…" I gasped as the vision of Brock's murderous glare returned to my mind.

Mrs. Wilton stroked my hair, patiently silent.

"I tried. I tried." The words choked in my throat. "I wanted to fight him, but I couldn't even stand up."

I blew my nose again, and swallowed my sobs. My eyes felt hot and puffy, but I straightened in the seat, and she handed me a fresh hanky as I drew in a calming breath. "I remember he shoved me down the stairs, and I landed on my hip. That's how it got bruised. I tried to push up from the floor, but Brock grabbed my arm and dragged me to his car. The pain in my shoulder was so…" Words escaped me. "I think I passed out again."

"When did you wake?"

"Not until the next morning. Actually, I think it was after noon. I was in my own bed."

Mrs. Wilton took hold of my trembling hands. "Do you remember what happened that day?"

I took a deep breath. "I didn't think about the party. Maybe it was because that drug was still in my system, or maybe I'd already pushed the memory away. It's weird, huh?"

Mrs. Wilton's steady eyes reached to me like an island shore in the midst of a storm-tossed sea. I latched onto the calm she offered and exhaled slowly. My tremors began to ease.

"I felt like I'd been sick for days. All I could think about was going home to Dad. Cheri came in and saw how ill I was. She suggested I take the bus home so I could rest on the way."

"Did Cheri see Brock bring you home that night?"

I shook my head. "She'd spent the night with friends at a different party."

"What about the bus trip? Do you remember that?"

I glanced aside, searching the fuzzy corners of my brain. "There isn't much to remember before arriving in Dalton. I must have slept a lot on the bus."

"And what about after you got back on the bus in Barrett?"

"Well…" My forehead wrinkled, as her question slowly registered in my mind. "What do you mean, Mrs. Wilton? I'm on that bus now—with you."

Her white brows rose. "Are you?"

Am I? Straightening in my seat, I looked around at the

sleeping passengers, gently rocking to the lullaby of the bus engine. What could she be talking about? This was the bus, with blowing snow streaking by the dark windows.

But the driver in front appeared as a mere silhouette against the glow of the dash lights, and in the dim light of the bus interior, the sleepers seemed unnaturally serene. I looked back to Mrs. Wilton. "Something isn't right here. What is it?"

"Have you been experiencing feelings of déjà vu these past few days?"

I dabbed my eyes and sat straight, my spine prickling. "Yes. Several times."

She tilted her head. "That's because all these events have already happened, my dear."

Mrs. Wilton seemed to be talking nonsense again. Just like when I first arrived at her inn.

"What are you talking about?"

"Everything from the time you arrived in Dalton is a memory being relived." She leaned toward me, looking over her glasses. "God has provided a chance for you to view these days again as if for the first time, so you could deal with the memories you hid away."

I swallowed, trying to absorb the implications. "But … all of this?"

She nodded, her steady eyes examining my face. "Remember the three words God told me to share with you while you were at the inn?"

Three words? She'd said many things, most of which I'd chalked up to her eccentricity. I shook my head. "Sorry."

"They were three words starting with 'R.'"

I flashed to our conversation at breakfast on the first morning after I'd arrived. "Oh yes. The first was 'Remember.'" The corner of my mouth rose at the realization I'd finally done that, with Mrs. Wilton's help.

"Good. You remember the things you had once hidden away. And those things which have been concealed from you are being revealed. The second word was—"

"Repent," I said it in unison with her.

"This opportunity is about to be put before you, and it will open the way for the last word to be accomplished. That word is …" She waited.

"Restore," I said. "But what do you mean about "repent" being an opportunity put before me?" I felt a prickling of the hair on my arms.

Mrs. Wilton pulled her crocheting bag up from the floor and tucked her handiwork inside. "You have one more memory yet to relive. This one will present your opportunity."

I clenched the fresh hanky she'd given me. *What more could there be?* "Are you sure? I recall everything now, except the parts when I was unconscious."

Mrs. Wilton folded her glasses and placed them in the top of her bag with a sigh. "I'm sorry to say you may find this memory to be the most difficult of all."

Brock had drugged me, assaulted me and threatened my life. What could she mean about something more difficult?

She put her hand on mine. "So far, you've focused on the things done to you." Her eyes were more piercing than

I'd ever seen. "But you must also remember the things you've done."

It all sounded so solemn. And final. "Mrs. Wilton, are you about to leave me? Please don't."

"Dear one, you are never alone."

"But what if this is too difficult for me?"

"When the Lord walks beside you, nothing is too difficult. I believe that is something your mother was fond of saying."

She was right. I could remember Mom lying on her bed, saying those very words. "Yeah. She did say that. I didn't believe it, though."

"And what about the other thing she always told you?"

"I don't know. What are you talking about?"

Even as I asked, it came back to me. Mom had said it over and over throughout her days with hospice. Even when her cheeks grew hollow. Even when she winced with pain.

All things work together for good. That's what she said, even when her breaths were too shallow to speak above a whisper.

It had become the phrase I took as firm evidence that faith was a lie that only served to delude its adherents.

TWENTY-SIX

The hospital room lights had been dimmed since sunset. Hope had just left to return home to Barrett, and Lance leaned toward a wall-mounted lamp beside Penny's bed. He held his Bible under the light.

"Here, I found it," he said gently. "It's Romans 8:28. 'And we know that all things work together for good to those who love God, to those who are called according to His purpose." He sat back in the chair and stretched a kink from his shoulder. "I remember how angry you were when I read that verse after your mom died, but do you remember it was her favorite verse? She said it over and over while she was battling the cancer and she held firm to it, even though I struggled."

He reached forward and placed his hand on Penny's head, gently stroking her brow with his thumb. "I didn't want to believe God was good anymore. In fact, I was sure He had abandoned us." The memory of that ache made Lance pause to bite his lip. "Your mom was right, though. I found out I had a lot of growing up to do and it started during those years when your mom fought her cancer battle. Lately, I've realized the troubles between you and me were another opportunity to grow, so I guess I'm still learning today. That's why I hold onto that verse now."

Lance leaned forward, his voice soft and low. "Sweetie, I don't know why the bus went off the road; whether Brock or some other lunatic caused the accident, or if it was just ice on the highway. I don't know what connection you may have to that murdered girl either, but I do believe your mom was right. God *is* able to use all things to do His good work. And many times, that good work is what's being done inside of us."

If Penny heard anything, she gave no sign of it. Only her steady breathing indicated she was alive.

Lance sat back in his chair. "I'm sorry you've been through so much without my help. I plan to do much better."

He flipped the pages of the Bible again, but tears blurred his vision. "We have a lot to do, you and me. Lots to make up for." He set the Bible aside and took her hand. "But we can do it. Come back to me, Penny. Let's make a fresh start, okay?"

"Mr. Doyle?" It was Hope, breathless at the door.

Surprised, Lance got up from his chair. "You forget something?"

Hope's eyes were wide. "I just saw Brock. He snuck into a room downstairs."

"He what?"

"He's up to something." Her voice cracked with anxiety. "I don't know what, but I'm sure it's not good."

Lance stood and moved quickly toward her. "What exactly did you see?"

"He had a duffle bag on his shoulder and at first he was facing away from me, studying his phone. Then he put it in his pocket and walked to a door midway down the hall. When he stopped at the door, I got nervous that he might see me, so I turned my back to him for a second, and the next time I looked, he was gone. I'm pretty sure he went into that other room."

"And you're sure it was him?"

She nodded.

"What floor?"

"Second. Room 211. There's a keypad beside that door, so maybe it's an office or a consultation room."

"He'd have to have the code to get in."

"Or watch someone else use the code," she countered.

"Can you stay here with Penny? I need to go find him."

"Sure." She raked a nervous hand through her short spiked hair. "I don't know what he's up to, but you should be careful."

She was right. He dashed down the hall and braced himself for the encounter as the elevator carried him down to the second floor.

A young gal was posted at the second floor desk. Lance leaned over the counter to pull her attention away from the monitor. "I'm looking for a young man about my height with dark, wavy hair. He's carrying a duffle bag and might be acting a little suspicious. Have you seen him?"

She shook her head. "Do I need to call security?"

It was a good idea—and one that reminded him he should notify Sergeant Clemens. "Sure. The cops have already talked to security about keeping an eye out for this guy, so tell them he's just been seen inside the building and that I've followed him to Room 211."

"And you are..." The girl's concern was overlaid with confusion.

"Dr. Lance Doyle."

She scribbled on a notepad, while picking up her phone.

Lance pulled out his own cell phone while moving toward the hallway intersection. A sign indicated Room 211 would be toward the back of the hospital. He punched Clemens' phone number and gazed down the corridor. He couldn't read the door numbers, but guessed it might be around the corner at the end of the hall.

The phone clicked as the line was picked up. "Sergeant Clemens."

"Hey, this is Lance Doyle. I've just learned that Brock Harper has returned to the hospital. Looks like he slipped past security somehow. I thought you'd want to know."

"Thanks. Can you find a way to keep him around until I can get there?"

"I have to find him first, but I'll try. Sorry to have to call you out so late."

"Not a problem. Besides, Maricopa County has just issued a warrant for him."

"A warrant?" His heartrate spiked. *Now what?*

"Yeah. Abbi Maxwell's boyfriend has been charged with her murder, and they want Harper brought in as an accessory."

Lance felt blood drain from his scalp. "You'd best hurry, then." He punched the phone's disconnect and went back to the receptionist at the hall desk. "Is security on the way?"

"He's helping a woman in the parking lot who locked herself out of—"

A surge of adrenaline drowned her voice out as it flooded Lance's system. He left the receptionist still talking and sprinted down the hall toward Room 211.

The girl called after him. "Doctor Doyle?"

He ignored her and kept moving. Had Brock learned about the warrant? What could Lance do or say to prevent him from leaving? A phlebotomy cart wheeled around the corner and Lance dodged around it before veering left. Room 211 was a few yards down on the right side.

This was it. With a deep breath, he strode to the door, took hold of the knob and tried to turn it. The door was locked. Of course. The keypad. He knocked. No answer. He rapped on it again, harder, then stepped back with a shake of his head. What now? Break the door down?

A voice to his left caught his attention. "What's going on here?" A matronly nurse with dark, slanted brows, stood several feet down the hall with hands on her ample hips. "I just chased someone out of that room, and now ... who are you people anyway?"

"Sorry. I'm looking for a young man with dark, wavy hair who was seen in this area. Is that the person you chased out?"

She ignored the question. "Seriously, who are you? I'll call security, if I must."

"He's already been called. He's out in the parking lot."

Undaunted, she stood her ground. "Perhaps that's the direction you should be going."

No point debating. He didn't belong here.

But then again, Brock might have gone out to the parking lot. If Lance hoped to detain him, he would need to move quickly. "Thanks, yes. I think I'll do that."

He race-walked back to the stairs and bounded down, two steps at a time. Once outside, he was struck by an icy breeze that swept along the sidewalk. He rubbed his arms and wished for his coat. Stepping out from the lighted portico, he peered across the dark lot. Rows of vehicles, uniformly grayed by slushy road grime, were hunched against the chill.

Not a single person was in sight. No security guy. No Brock. Lance picked his way across the frozen slush, scanning down the rows. He caught sight of an SUV down one row and jogged over for a closer look but it had Colorado plates. Another one caught his eye but turned out to be a different model.

Lance huffed a breath into the cold night air. It looked like Brock had managed to disappear again. Headlights skimmed across the lot as a vehicle behind him turned onto the property. He looked over his shoulder as a dark car straightened onto a different driveway—one that angled toward the back of the hospital. It looked like a dark Toyota, but was it Brock's? All he knew for certain was that Brock's car wasn't in the lot where he stood. He might as well check it out. Rubbing his hands together briskly before shoving them in his pockets, he headed back across the driveway.

Sierra Memorial wasn't a large complex but it still took a couple minutes to get around to the back of the building. When the walkway ended at a side door, he maneuvered through some shrubbery, piled snow and concrete barriers to access another path that would lead the right direction.

Panting, he stopped after rounding the building's back corner. The Emergency Department entrance angled from an extension at the back of the building. A few vehicles were parked in a small lot adjacent to its automatic doors. None were Brock's. Another lane resembling an alley proceeded beyond the ER. He jogged toward it, crossing the street and bypassing the curbside pull-up in front of the Emergency doors.

Upon reaching the far corner of the building extension, Lance stopped. The alley was clearly a utility access for service vehicles and personnel. Would Brock have gone down this lane? He looked back at the parking area, nearly deserted. There were no other places the vehicle could have gone.

He jogged down the alley to the far end of the ground level extension and stopped short when the alley widened. There was Brock's car tucked around the corner against the brick wall. Empty.

A utility access ladder was mounted to the wall above the car. Had Brock used the car as a way to reach the ladder? It sure appeared that way, but why would he go up on the roof of the ER? Where could he go from there?

A quick glance around showed no other viable options. Only trash bins and caged utility meters. Brock must have gone up on the roof.

Equally perplexing was the presence of a partial jug of antifreeze that sat on the ground next to the car, as if the guy had stopped to take time to refill his windshield washers before climbing the ladder. Strange.

What on earth was Brock up to? Lance rubbed the chill from his arms. Perhaps he thought he could get back into Room 211 from the roof. That room was accessible from there, though it didn't explain why he should want to be in that room.

Unfortunately, time was wasting. At a loss for answers, Lance climbed onto the hood of Brock's car, then scrambled up the windshield to reach the car's roof. He reached for the ladder and stretched to get his foot on the lowest rung, wishing he had worn shoes with better traction.

Nevertheless, he began the climb.

Whatever Brock was up to, it was time to bring it to an end.

TWENTY-SEVEN

What was going on? I swiveled in my seat and looked around me. Mrs. Wilton said nothing more as I stood slowly and stepped into the aisle. Something felt oddly different about the bus. Could this be merely a memory as Mrs. Wilton had suggested?

Many of the passengers surrounding me were still sleeping, but not all. The man in the back row near the bathroom held a book under his dome light, reading. His head bobbed slightly with the movement of the bus. A teen boy immediately behind me glanced up from a game he played on his phone. I offered a smile, but he returned to the game without reciprocating. The otherworldly sensation I'd felt moments ago had faded, and the atmosphere of the bus seemed natural again. If only I could pinpoint the source of my initial eeriness. Was it something to do with the engine noise? Or the motion created by the bus suspension?

"Mrs. Wilton—" I turned back to her seat, but she was gone. Instead, the coat I had discarded before my panic attack in the bathroom lay on the spot where she had sat, as if she'd never been there at all. Had I just awakened from a vivid dream? Feeling suddenly self-conscious, I slid back down onto the seat.

Mrs. Wilton said I had one more memory to relive. I pulled the coat onto my lap and considered her words, but nothing about my current situation seemed to have been repeated. I felt no strange sensations of déjà vu. What could I be reliving? I was sitting on a bus headed toward home. It was happening right now. I checked my watch—11:37. My ticket said we would arrive in Clearmont at 12:30. Less than an hour away.

Maybe my overstressed mind had taken Mrs. Wilton's off-kilter personality to the next level. The notion she was an angel was as silly as her idea about this whole trip having already happened. So far-fetched it made me uneasy. Why couldn't I just relax, take this last hour to rest and prepare for arriving back home?

Why? Because I'd cried in her lap while she held my hand. We had talked. I'd felt her arm around my shoulder and her warm hand resting on my head while she prayed.

All that had been so very real, but then, without warning, she had disappeared.

I closed my eyes. *Now who's going a little batty?*

A faint, yet harsh noise emanated from somewhere behind the bus. As the noise repeated, increasing in volume, more passengers woke. First a long blaring note followed by two or three short hostile blasts. A car horn.

A man behind me smudged his sleeve against the window to wipe away condensation. He pressed his face to the glass while a baby began to cry in another part of the bus. Others also shifted uncomfortably with the disruption.

The harsh tones repeated as insistent as ever, growing louder as the vehicle neared.

"It's that guy again," the window-looker said.

"Oh man," someone else moaned.

The woman in the seat across the aisle looked my way, her lips taut, as if I were responsible for the noisy interruption.

I clenched my coat in a panic. Brock was back, and judging by the horn blares, he was angry. This insanity had to end, but how? I cringed at the thought of Brock's gun.

If only I could reason with the driver. Convince him to stay ahead of Brock and avoid another confrontation.

I leapt up and my coat dropped, crumpling to the floor. "Keep going!" I shouted to the driver. He didn't seem to hear me. I half-stumbled and trampled over the coat in my rush to the front of the bus.

Brock's horn sounded again. He was in the left lane.

I yelled again, "Don't stop!"

Was the driver ignoring me? His forehead, reflected in the rear-view mirror above him, was lined with concern while he glanced repeatedly out the side window.

Brock's headlights slowly advanced beside the bus. In a final lurch forward, I grabbed the support pole behind the driver's seat and pulled myself against it. "Driver, please." I leaned in over his shoulder. "He'll kill me if you stop."

"What're you talking about?" He yelled above the sound of Brock's angry car horn.

"He's got a gun."

"Get back from here. It's not safe."

"Don't stop. Please. I'm begging you."

"He's passing us," the driver barked. "Now move back. I'm telling ya, it's not safe."

"But he'll stop the bus again." I grabbed at his shoulder.

He tugged away.

Then someone grabbed me from behind and pulled me back with his arm around my waist. I gripped the pole with one hand and pried at the stranger's fingers with the other. "Let me go!"

Was this New Year's Eve all over again? It seemed I was trapped in another desperate battle against Brock's brawn, but this time my hands were not limp. My legs didn't collapse. This time I could claw and scream. "Let. Me. Go!"

Clasping my hands together for added strength, I jabbed one elbow back as hard as I could. My attacker's grip loosened, and I twisted out of his grasp. Spinning around, I lost my balance and staggered backward against the bus console. The back of my head smacked the windshield.

The bus driver threw an angry glance my way and pointed his finger. "Lady, you gotta get back and sit down now!"

Brock's headlights came into view through the window beside the driver. He was coming to kill me. I could feel his fury in the horn's incessant blast.

The driver noted his approach and took his foot off the accelerator.

"No!" I screamed and grabbed hold of the steering wheel. "He'll kill me!"

Immediate horror flooded my senses as the bus careened wildly on the icy road. We both held our grip on the wheel, jolting one direction, then another. Screams filled the cabin. My ribs smacked against the console repeatedly.

The driver pressed the brakes and I lost my grip on the wheel. The bus fishtailed and I slid sideways, tumbling down the steps. I landed against the exit door as the entire vehicle tilted. Metal screeched and groaned. Panicked voices shrieked with mine—a horrified chorus. Glass rained down in exploded bits. I groped for something, anything to brace myself, then felt a momentary weightlessness just before a ghastly crunch and everything went black.

TWENTY-EIGHT

Lance reached the top of the utility access ladder and climbed over the low parapet that wrapped around the first floor Emergency Department. He stood a moment to catch his breath. No need to wonder where Brock had gone. Footprints punctured the snow, leading from where he stood straight across the flat rooftop toward the main building. A moment later, he spotted a window slightly ajar. It was about ten feet above the ER roof, and a rope hung from it with a few knots tied at intervals.

It had all the hallmarks of some covert spy operation. What on earth was Brock up to?

No time to ponder the unfathomable. Lance raced as fast as his slick-soled shoes would allow, following Brock's path. Upon reaching the rope, he gave it a sharp tug. It felt secure enough, and the fall risk was minimal.

Gripping the rope, he pulled up until he could pry the fingers of one hand into the gap at the bottom of the sash. Would Brock see him trying to get in? It was possible, but Lance refused to dwell on it. He had to get inside.

Initially, the window resisted his efforts. Numbing cold didn't help, but once he edged the sash open a bit more, he got a solid grip and proper leverage with his arm. A few more moments and he'd lifted himself enough to look inside. Relieved to find Brock was nowhere in sight, he pulled up until he managed to get a knee onto the sill.

Lance worked to quietly nudge the window sash higher and get himself over the ledge. No telling what might happen if that hostile nurse reappeared.

Fortunately, the interior segment of his unplanned escapade was comparatively easy, the floor being only a short step down from the sill. He lowered the window sash and noticed Brock's rope had been secured to the base of a tall locker cabinet nearby. The cabinet, part of a long row of lockers, made it clear this was a staff changing room.

Lance hurried to the far end of the row and checked both directions. Another aisle of lockers and a laundry cart were on the right. Had Brock come here in hopes of impersonating a member of hospital staff?

No time to worry about Brock's motives. He had to catch up to the young man. Quietly, Lance slipped out the exit door and jogged back toward the elevators.

Stopping at the nurse's desk, he cleared his throat.

"May I—?" The girl began, then interrupted herself when she looked up from the monitor. "Oh, it's you."

"I need immediate assistance." He grabbed a pen and began to jot a note. "My daughter's a patient in Room 338, and I need your security personnel to meet me there. Here's my number."

Her eyebrows rose. "And what should I tell him?"

"The young man I told you about—my height, dark hair, duffle bag?"

The girl nodded.

"There's a warrant for his arrest, and I believe he's headed to my daughter's room right now. Police are on the way, but I may need help to restrain him. Please send your guys to Room 338."

He didn't wait for a reply, but dashed to the stairwell, his wet shoes skidding on the tile. Panting, he bounded up to the third floor.

A duty nurse with an armload of linens side-stepped as he passed by. "In a hurry, Dr. Doyle?"

Lance spun on his heel to face her. "Have you seen the young man who visited Penny early this morning?"

"I thought he left."

"He's been seen again, and the police are on their way."

The nurse pulled back. "Oh?"

He moved away with a wave of his hand. "Send them to Penny's room."

"Is everything all right?"

Lance would have answered but he was already taking long strides down the corridor. If Brock discovered the police were coming, it would be difficult to prevent him from leaving. Hopefully, Clemens would arrive soon.

Lance's heart pounded in his chest. It would do no good to rush in or be confrontational. Better to stay calm. Don't question him about the locker room. Keep him focused on Penny. Encourage him to stick around for her sake. Anything that might keep him off-guard to the arrival of authorities.

Lance rounded the corner at the end of the hall, and an odd sound alerted him. It came from Penny's room. Then a scuffle and hard thud were accompanied by a brief shriek. Did someone fall to the floor? Penny?

He sprinted the last few yards and grabbed the doorframe, skidding into Penny's room.

At first glance, nothing seemed amiss—except that Penny's bed was positioned at an odd angle. Why was it moved? Penny lay on it just as he had last seen her after the surgery, except her head now tilted to one side and it appeared her eyes might be slightly open. Had she been moving around in the bed? Getting nearer to consciousness?

What's this? A large syringe, filled with a pale blue liquid, stood on end, punctured into Penny's IV port inches from her hand. Had Brock added something to her Ringer's lactate solution?

Could it be the antifreeze he'd seen outside Brock's car?

Lance rushed toward her, but came to an abrupt halt when, from the far side of the bed, a figure in a white lab coat rose up from hiding and rotated toward him. Brock, dressed in a coat he'd undoubtedly pilfered from the locker room's laundry bin. He held Hope clutched against his chest with a hand over her mouth while she struggled in vain against his muscular grip.

Seeing Lance, Hope stopped struggling, but her eyes remained wide with fear.

Brock's expression was grim, his hair in loose disarray over a determined brow. He spoke into Hope's ear while keeping his eyes on Lance. "Don't make a peep," he snarled.

Lance's pulse raced. He took a hesitant step toward them. "What's going on, and what have you done to Penny's IV?"

Brock raised his other hand, which gripped a pocket knife. "Don't come any closer."

"Brock." Lance shook his head. *God, help me. What should I say?* "I don't know what brought all this on, but this … this can't end well. You have to stop now."

Brock's eyes darted back and forth. "Shut up. You don't know anything."

"Think, man. What will this solve?"

"There's nothing to solve."

"Sure there is. You're stressed out, but this—" Lance indicated the knife gripped in Brock's hand. "This isn't necessary. Let me remove that syringe and we'll talk this through, figure it out." Brock's fiery eyes strayed toward Penny, but Lance couldn't discern the look. "Something happened between you and Penny. Tell me. I can help you."

"It's none of your business."

"Brock, it's going to be everybody's business if you don't relax and put a stop to this." Slowly, he took another step toward them.

Brock looked him in the eye, and pressed the knife edge against Hope's neck. "I already warned you. Stay back."

Lance stopped and forced his arms to relax. "What do you want to do, Brock?"

Brock seemed to consider the question. Hope's eyes shifted, craning to see Brock's reaction.

Behind Lance, footsteps rounded through the doorway. He glanced over his shoulder as a man in uniform entered and stopped short.

Hospital security.

TWENTY-NINE

A warm hand pressed my neck, making me aware of the chilly air. "Over here," an unfamiliar voice called from a distance. The hand lifted and footsteps moved toward the distant voice.

Snowflakes landed on my cheek. I was outside.

I'd been on a bus. What happened? I took a deep breath and eased my eyes open to the midnight darkness of a snowy wood. I was numb with cold. Attempting to lift my head, I gasped with immediate pain. Something was wrong with my head or my neck. Maybe both.

I tried to judge my body's position. I seemed to be mostly face down, but on uneven ground with my legs bent oddly. My right arm was pinned under me, a possible cause for the sharp pain in my ribs that accompanied each breath. With painstaking slowness, I managed to shift one of my legs, thankful at the realization I wasn't paralyzed. That slight adjustment also eased the pain of breathing. I drew in cold air and exhaled white vapor.

Where was the bus? I couldn't tell, but somewhere behind me I could detect a child's whimper. More sounds indicated people stirring or in pain. There must have been an accident. Someone walked among us, talking softly. Probably calling for an ambulance.

I could move my left arm, the pain tolerable. I reached up to calm my pulse-aching head, but the barest touch felt like fire. I pulled my hand back, and under the shadow of the pines, it shone black with sticky blood.

After wiping it on my thigh, I reached to push aside the snow that blocked my view.

The bus driver's grey face, less than a yard from my own, took my breath away. He lay in a pool of blood, staring with lifeless eyes.

I pinched mine shut. *Oh God. Please.* Too late. The ghoulish image had etched itself in my mind.

The last terrible moments of my screaming tirade rushed back to memory … the fight … clawing at the stranger's hands … yelling at the driver and finally … grabbing the wheel.

No, no. In some kind of crazed panic, it seemed I'd lost all self-control. My recklessness had brought all this suffering. It was my fault—mine alone—that the bus had rolled off the road.

I had killed this man and who knows how many others.

I drew my arm up in front of my face in a feeble attempt to shut out the horror. An agonized groan emerged from my throat.

What was it Mrs. Wilton had said? She'd warned me, but this was far worse than anything I might have imagined. She had reminded me that God's second word for me was "repent," but no apology could make up for this.

Instead of receiving forgiveness, my admission of guilt would only put me in line for harsh justice from a God who, by now, had certainly given up on me.

My vision blurred, and I closed my eyes. I blinked when unknown hands laid a covering around my shoulders. "Help is coming," a female voice spoke softly. "Just hold on." She pressed a cloth to my head. I anticipated a sting, but my senses had dulled.

My eyelids drooped.

The woman stood and called out, "This one's lost a lot of blood."

No one answered her. Perhaps they were dying too. Or dead already.

She crouched back down and pressed the cloth to my head. Her voice was muffled, indistinct. It seemed as though her touch reached me from a great distance. I wasn't cold anymore. My life was fading. It grew thinner with each breath.

"Let me die." I mouthed the words and drifted into warm darkness.

THIRTY

B rock's eyes grew wide with the appearance of the security guard.

Lance raised his hand to halt the guard's entry but kept his eyes on Brock. Given the current situation, it was difficult to say whether a uniformed presence would be beneficial or a hindrance. He didn't want to take a chance at further escalating the situation. Fortunately, it didn't appear that any of the blue liquid had been injected into Penny's IV, though some might seep into the line if it stayed in the port.

"What's going on?" the guard called from the doorway.

Lance nodded toward Brock. "My friend is under a lot of stress. We were discussing ways to alleviate it."

Taking a breath, Lance raised his hands with palms out. "Listen to me, Brock. I'm going to pull that syringe out of the IV. I want you to think long and hard before you do anything more. Things will only get worse, if you continue."

Brock's gaze shifted to the guard and back. "Neither of you know anything," he snarled.

"I know about Abbi Maxwell."

Brock's eyes registered momentary surprise, but he didn't reply.

"I know about your friend too. What was his name again?"

Brock shook his head. "It doesn't matter. His dreams and mine are both going down the toilet."

"If anyone else gets hurt, it'll only become worse. There's no need to destroy your whole life." Lance edged up to Penny's bed, and reached toward the IV line.

"You know how many scouts have been out there watching us?" Brock's knuckles were white from gripping the knife. "We're the Dynamic Duo. Tyler's been the top college quarterback in the division for two years now. He could even be a first round draft pick."

"I know it's hard, but listen to me, Brock. Your life is not over. You need to make a wise choice right now." Lance grasped the IV line and pulled it toward him, sliding his hand toward the injection port.

Brock clamped his mouth shut. Beads of perspiration appeared on his forehead. "It's all Tyler's fault."

"I know." Lance grasped the base of the syringe and carefully pulled it from the line. He stepped back from the bed with his hands still raised. Sympathy might help gain Brock's confidence. "Look. There's no need to take this any further, right? Put down the knife, and let us deal with Tyler."

Brock's gaze shifted to the floor. He shook his head. Disagreement? Regret? Lance couldn't tell. "Talk to me, Brock. Tell me what you're thinking. Together, we can figure this out."

The guard's walkie-talkie crackled. A voice emanated from his shoulder comm. "Officers on site."

The guard clicked the comm with his thumb. "Room 338."

"Hear that? It's over, Brock." Lance extended an open hand. "Let me have the knife."

Brock worked his jaw in silence.

Movement from the bed, caught Lance's attention. Penny lifted a limp hand up an inch or two off the blanket. Her fingers slowly straightened and wiggled for a few shaky moments before dropping again to the bed. Then a flutter of eyelash movement. Was she waking up?

Brock's expression registered alarm. "Both of you," he barked abruptly, "Over to the window."

Lance shifted his eyes toward the guard who nodded. They both edged away from the door.

"Over against the window!" Brock's eyes glared with new intensity. He grasped Hope tight to his chest and maneuvered swiftly around the end of Penny's bed. With a final hard shove, he flung the young woman toward the men and bolted for the door.

Hope sprawled to the floor with a shriek, and Lance launched himself in Brock's direction. Leaping over Hope, he stretched forward to grasp Brock's arm.

The football champ leaned forward to muscle through Lance's tackle attempt. With a harsh jerk, he wrenched his arm from Lance's grip.

Lance gritted his teeth. He couldn't let Brock manage another disappearing act. Not when armed officers were so close. As he fell to the floor, his arm slid against the back of

Brock's leg and, a second later, his hand caught hold of Brock's heel. *Hold on!*

The wide receiver twisted out of Lance's grip, tumbling to the floor in the process. He rolled on his shoulder and hopped back to his feet. Fortunately, the hospital security officer smacked into his side with a grunt that sent them both sliding against the door frame.

Lance pulled himself up on all fours, panting, and joined the security officer who swiftly tugged a pair of handcuffs from a pouch on his belt. Together they secured Brock's hands behind his back and got him seated on the floor with his back against the door.

With great effort, Lance stood to his feet, panting. Hope had gone to Penny's bedside and he joined her there, turning his attention to his daughter.

"I thought sure she was waking up," Hope said.

Carefully, Lance lifted an eyelid and studied Penny's pupils. They remained unfocused. Though he was glad Penny had managed to move her hand briefly, it appeared she was still locked away inside her mind. "She might be partially aware, at least some of the time."

Deputies arrived at the door and, together with the security guard, stood Brock to his feet and led him out of the room. One officer stayed to question Hope, who leaned against the wall with a hand on her forehead.

"I was in the bathroom when he arrived," she said. "I could hear someone was in the room, but I thought it was one of the nurses. I didn't realize it was Brock until I opened the door."

Lance studied her from his place beside Penny's bed.

Hope's features were pale and drawn. He went to her. "I shouldn't have left you alone here. I had no idea how desperate Brock was."

Hope slid onto a nearby chair, her lip quivering. "Who could have guessed he would want to kill her?"

The deputy scratched notes on his tablet. "Do either of you have any idea what his motive might have been?"

Lance answered. "No, but he may have been under a lot of pressure from his so-called friend. Sounds like they both stood to lose a great deal if they were implicated in the other girl's death."

After the last officer left, Lance returned to Penny's side and caressed his daughter's forehead. Her eyes were closed and her hands rested on the blanket, unmoving. He glanced to Hope, who remained in the chair against the wall. "Perhaps Penny knew about their role in the other girl's death. Maybe that's why she was trying to get home."

"If she knew anything, she didn't tell me about it." Hope leaned forward to prop her head in her hands. "When I saw that Brock was going to inject something into her IV, all I could do was yell at him." Her voice cracked. "He turned on me and everything escalated to a blur."

Lance searched Penny's arms, hands and face. "It doesn't appear that he pierced her skin anywhere. He must have believed an injection through the IV would go unnoticed. Did he hurt you, Hope?"

"No. Just a few bruises."

Lance marveled at the young woman who had saved

his daughter's life. He owed her a debt of gratitude. "You acted bravely. I don't quite know how to thank you."

"You just did."

"Well, take your time and rest. Nice even breaths until your heart slows. Everything's going to be fine."

Lance took hold of Penny's hand and bent to kiss her brow. "I'm back again, Penny, and I know you're close. Can you hear me?"

Her eyelashes trembled for a moment, but when he lifted the lids, the pupils remained unfocused.

"Don't worry, Penny. You're doing great. If you can hear me at all, squeeze my hand.

Nothing.

Lance sighed. "Come back to me, sweetie. I'm right here."

THIRTY-ONE

Sunshine warmed my shoulders as I sauntered up the driveway. I skimmed my hand over the prickly top of Dad's carefully pruned waist-high boxwood hedge. At the far end, angled beside the corner of the garage, stood Mom's white-painted arbor covered with purple clematis.

But something wasn't quite right. A slightly unnatural sensation, like the one I'd felt on the bus, niggled at my brain. I slowed my pace, uncertain. I'd finally made it home, but how did I get here? In spite of everything I'd experienced in the last few days, my memories continued to be fuzzy.

A light breeze made the blooms on the arbor shiver. It teased at the loose ends of my hair. Busy insects and small bird chatter filled my senses. All so real, and yet not quite real at all.

Mrs. Wilton had said God gave me a chance to relive past events in order to remember, repent, and restore. Was I still reliving the past? How could I know for sure? And if this wasn't part of my past experience, what was it?

In an abrupt flash, the grating screech and grind of the rolling bus crashed through my fragile senses. Clasping hands over my ears, I doubled over while attempting to shut out the horror of it. I remembered the crisp icy cold of waking on the snowy hillside. The warmth of hands ministering to my wounds. Then the sight of the bus driver's bloodied face that sent a renewed pang deep into my chest.

Gratefully, the vision ended, and I opened my eyes again to the warmth and sunshine of home. How could I have ever pushed those memories aside? People had died, and I was responsible.

Even more perplexing was the fact I had been transported from that horrific scene and brought here, where everything seemed pristine and my injuries healed.

Perhaps I was dreaming. Or in some kind of afterlife. Some in-between limbo designed for people God hadn't made up His mind about.

A murmuring sound reached my ears. It came from the arbor—or maybe the patio alcove beyond. Voices perhaps?

I crept closer, and the faint sounds continued. Why so muted? Were people conversing inside the house or further off—in a neighboring yard?

When I reached the white painted arch, the sounds stopped. Utter silence. I leaned in to listen. Seeing Mom's little patio garden after such a long absence warmed me. Beautiful bright flowers sprouted from a variety of arranged pots, and the perimeter hedged by the boxwoods sheltered a small seating nook with a café table and chairs.

So lovely, but … still wrong, somehow.

Of course. In the real world, it was January, the holiday

break from school. This summery vision couldn't possibly be real.

I entered the space, and the murmur of voices resumed.

I strained to filter the soft vocal babble, until one voice emerged apart from the rest. It was Dad, his words faintly carried on the wind. "Come back to me, Penny."

"Dad?"

"I'm right here."

I twirled in the alcove, eyes raised to study the sky. "Where are you?"

"Come back, sweetie."

"But I can't find you."

A knot choked my throat and I lowered my head. My eyes landed on the front door—the same door I had visualized so many times on this trip. If this were some kind of afterlife, then maybe Mom was here ready to greet me inside. Perhaps … I took a step. Then another.

But one step away from the door, I knew the truth. Mom wasn't here, and this place, however lovely, wasn't really my home or any kind of afterlife. Maybe it wasn't even possible to get home from here.

That thought sunk into my gut like a stone.

I stared at the door, realizing that the thing I really wanted—that I especially needed right now—was my Dad. I had always blamed him for how we grew so far apart, but all along I had been the one continually pushing away.

"I'm sorry, Dad. Can you forgive me?" If only he could, but I had no confidence he could even hear me.

Another phantom of his voice carried in on the warm

summer breeze. "Come back to me, Penny." Though faint, it was filled with emotion. With longing. As if he wanted me as much as I wanted him.

I took the final step and stood before the door. After a moment's hesitation, I pressed the bell. The familiar chime sounded inside.

I stared at the knob. "Dad? Are you there?" I placed my palm against the door. My voice cracked. "I want to come home."

Then, without warning, the knob turned and the door swung wide.

Dad stood in the doorway and his face quickly transformed with surprised delight. "Penny!" He rushed to wrap his arms around me, and a sudden wave of intense warmth flowed from my chest out through my entire body. A tingling, energizing warmth that filled every cell, as if suddenly waking from numbness.

I slumped into Dad's embrace, but he held me up. He squeezed me repeatedly like Mom used to do. "Penny, Penny, Penny." He said my name over and over.

Then the bright flower-filled alcove, the front door, and the entire house dissolved away.

It didn't matter. Dad still held me. He still cried my name.

I was lying on a bed in an unfamiliar room, gathered up in my father's embrace.

"Everything is fine now, sweetie. You're going to be okay." He heaved a great sigh and lowered my head and shoulders onto the bed. "Sorry. I know how bruised you are, but I'm so glad you've come back."

THIRTY-TWO

Water trickled down the face of the canyon wall in rivulets as Dad drove Hope and me over the mountain pass toward Dalton. It dripped from rock ledges and spilled from tiny crevices, each dribble joining with others to create a sparkling, joyous cascade. Five months ago, I had traveled the opposite direction on this road, with Brock at the wheel and an avalanche of emotional conflict and uncertainty ahead. What a major course change my life had taken since.

Dad and Hope's conversation seemed to mimic the sounds of the trickling stream that followed the road bed. Their voices receded to the background as I considered how that earlier journey had been prompted by some unrecognized inner drive. Would I have come to this place of healing without experiencing all that had led me here? Perhaps every element of joy and pain had been necessary. At the very least, God had found it useful as He gently prodded me back to a more centered life.

The cascade of events that began along this road had resulted in a major thaw, not only in my relationship with Dad, but with God as well.

Without intending to, I spoke my thoughts aloud. "This is where it happened."

Hope leaned forward from the back seat. "What's that?"

I shook my head. "Sorry, I didn't mean to interrupt. I guess my mind was wandering."

"No, I've been chattering endlessly since you picked me up." She patted my shoulder. "What happened here?"

I shifted sideways in the seat. "Somewhere along this road is where I realized my relationship with Brock might be ending."

Hope's eyes softened. "That was a rough day for you."

"Yeah, it was." My thoughts flicked to the bus crash, but the heart-piercing memory of those who perished kept me from lingering there. "I have to try to focus on the good that has come from it."

Dad glanced toward me. "I wish you hadn't had to go through so much. I should have tried harder." He'd repeated this sentiment many times since I first awoke in the hospital.

I patted his arm. "Apparently, it's what I needed to go through. And it wasn't all bad." I shifted toward Hope. "I made a new friend that day."

She smiled back. "Me too."

Hope's friendship had helped speed my recovery, so mere thanks seemed inadequate. My head injury was healing well and with very little residual effect. My broken bones and bruises had also required time and rest, but physical therapy was keeping me on track to a complete recovery. And through it all, my appreciation for Hope had grown. She helped rejuvenate my spirit and encouraged the ongoing emotional healing between Dad and me.

Hope spoke up. "So, is there a decent restaurant in Dalton? I'm going to be hungry."

"Yeah." I paused while searching my memory. "*Café du Louvre*. That's the place." I looked over my shoulder to Hope. "You'll be happy to know they have great pie."

Hope pressed an index finger into her cheek with a conspiratorial grin. "Hmmm … really?" As usual, she made me giggle.

Dad looked confused. "What?"

We answered Hope's favorite mantra in unison. "Pie fixes everything."

Dad's expression suggested doubt.

I visualized the quaint little town that lay a few miles ahead. "It's right across the street from Mrs. Wilton's inn."

More than the café, I was especially eager to visit the inn and see Mrs. Wilton again. I'd made a couple attempts to get a contact number for her during my recovery, but without success. It didn't worry me. She wouldn't mind us dropping in unannounced. After all, that's how I'd first met her.

Dad slowed to navigate a switchback. "Maybe we should invite Mrs. Wilton to join us for lunch at the café."

"That's a great idea."

Hope leaned forward between the seats. "I hate to revive the subject of Brock, but have you heard any recent updates about the murder case in Phoenix?"

Dad glanced toward her in the rear-view mirror. "Not much more since we last spoke. They've both been charged with multiple counts having to do with the drugs and Abbi's death. A trial date will probably be set in the next few months."

Hope shifted her gaze to me. "How do you feel about that?"

"I'm not looking forward to testifying—or facing Brock again. It's important, though. I have to tell them what I remember."

Brock had been shifting as much blame as he could on Tyler since his arrest. Was it just a tactic he hoped would work in his favor? I wasn't certain about much except that they had conspired together to drug each of us on New Year's Eve and take advantage of the drug's memory-dampening effects. The plan might have worked, had Abbi not accidently drunk part of my dose. That unanticipated slipup had left me somewhat cognizant of the night's events and doomed her with a fatal overdose.

Dad shifted to a lower gear. "I suspect you're more worried about your own court date."

"I'm trying not to stress about it." Trying didn't make it easy though, and glancing toward Dad, I knew he was worried too. We had discussed the bus crash many times during my recovery. God had told me to remember, repent, and restore. The old me would have balked, but I intended to follow through. After facing the memories I'd hidden away, I knew I had to also face my actions and continue the process of restoration. How else could I hope to make things right?

Hope sighed. "I don't know how you do it, Penny. You're so much stronger than me."

Was I strong? Vehicular manslaughter was an ominous charge to face, but I had gone before the judge believing the truth was better than a lie. The facts had been laid on the table, and at the time, it struck me as being akin to putting myself on an ancient sacrificial altar. It hadn't proved fatal, as it did with Old Testament lambs, but the proverbial hatchet would fall with the strike of a gavel next week. I would have to accept whatever judgment came.

I certainly didn't feel strong, and jail time seemed likely, though my lawyer believed the extenuating circumstances might help promote leniency.

The imminent prospect of incarceration had prompted my desire to make this trip to Dalton. I hoped Mrs. Wilton would help me find peace with what lay ahead.

I shook my head. "I'm not any stronger than you, or anyone else. I just want to do the right thing."

Before long, the valley opened ahead of us and we reached Dalton in the early afternoon. Everything was just as I remembered, only fresh and bright with the renewal of spring. We pulled around the corner off the highway, and I saw the sloping embankment Kitty made me climb the first night I arrived. The black rooftop and dormers of the inn were visible beyond its crest.

I pointed. "The driveway entrance is farther up the hill."

"And this?" Hope indicated the storefront on her side of the car.

"Oh, yes. That's the café."

She tilted her head. "It's cute, in a rustic sort of way."

"Well, I suppose it's not exactly the *Piece de Resistance*, but—" We both giggled at the reference to Hope's employer.

Dad cut in. "We're going to Mrs. Wilton's inn first, right?"

"Yes, yes." I looked up the street and spotted workers setting twin posts along the embankment. "Looks like Mrs. Wilton is getting a sign put up. Good for her."

We turned onto the long cobbled driveway and Dad stopped the car in front of the walkway leading to the front door. By the look of things, Mrs. Wilton had been busy. The overgrown landscaping was pruned and reworked with new shrubs and flowers planted along the sidewalk. The lawn was greening up with the help of a wide-fanning sprinkler. The house itself hardly resembled the foreboding structure I remembered.

I was half out of the vehicle by the time Dad shut off the engine. "Would you look at this?" I exclaimed. "She's getting this place really spruced up."

I dashed up the walkway and bounded the stairs while Dad and Hope climbed out to stand beside the car. Rapping the door-knocker, I stood in breathless anticipation.

A middle-aged woman in paint-spattered coveralls opened the door. Beyond her, the lion head atop the stair post gleamed with fresh polish. I recalled the times I had patted its head.

"Hello," I said. "My name's Penny."

"Hello." She smiled brightly. "You must be the interior decorator. I'm Janet."

"No." It came out sounding more like a question.

"Oh?" Her brows arched. "You're not here about the wallpaper?"

An uneasy feeling crept up my spine. "I'm a friend of Mrs. Wilton. I just stopped by for a quick visit. That is, if she's home."

"I'm sorry. Are you sure you have the correct address?"

"Oh yes. I was here in January."

The woman's expression changed. "I'm not sure how that's possible. This house was closed up last summer after the owner died. No one's been here until we purchased it last month." She called over her shoulder. "Lonnie? What was the previous owner's name?"

A man came to the door, wiping his hands on a rag. "Hi there."

Janet brushed at some sawdust on his shoulder. "This girl is looking for someone. Perhaps a relative of the previous owner. What was the old man's name again?"

"Let me think..." His mouth twisted as his eyes skimmed above the doorframe. "I'm sure it'll come to me. It was ... Wilton Burgess."

Janet looked at me with surprise. "Didn't you just say 'Wilton'?"

I swallowed. "Yes, uh..." But what did this mean? I glanced over my shoulder at Dad and Hope, still waiting by the car. Had Mrs. Wilton been some figment of my imagination? Gloom formed a lump in my chest. "Thank you for your help." I swallowed again, but the lump remained. "I think you're right. It seems I've made a mistake."

I trudged back to the car while watching Dad's gaze shift from expectancy to confusion.

Hope put on a hand on my shoulder. "What's wrong?"

"Mrs. Wilton doesn't live here."

She pulled back. "Oh no. Did she die?"

"I don't think she ever lived here."

Dad moved to open the car door. "Let's go. You can tell us about it on the way to the café."

I wasn't sure what I could tell them. They'd already heard the full account of my journey and how I'd relived so many memories during my coma. Mrs. Wilton was an essential part of those memories, and everything I experienced had lined up with fact … except her.

Hope guided me to sit in the backseat next to her. "So, what did they say?"

"They just bought the house from the estate of an old man named Wilton Burgess. They've never heard of Mrs. Wilton."

"That's odd."

"There's more. They said the house was closed up all winter, but I know I stayed there—two nights. I saw the carved lion's head inside the door." Anxiety was turning to frustration in my voice. "It's no figment of my imagination. I was there."

Dad stopped at the end of the driveway and looked at my reflection in the rear view mirror. "You told me she claimed to be an angel."

"I know, but she said lots of strange things. That was only one of them."

"Even so…" He pulled onto the road. "For weeks,

you've been telling me how each part of your journey seemed to happen by God's intervention. Should it surprise you that Mrs. Wilton was God's intervention too?"

As he pulled into a parking space in front of the café, I had to agree. Whether real or not, she had been a Godsend. A quirky, funny, irreplaceable reminder that He cared for me. Still, if she wasn't real, how had I been inside that old house?

We entered the café, which cheerfully buzzed with customers. Its familiar charm warmed me. I took comfort in the fact that at least this part of my time in Dalton was just as I remembered it.

While taking our seats at a vacant table, I pointed out the scenic landscape paintings on the walls around the room. "The owner here sells her artwork. Isn't it—" My eyes stopped at the booth directly across from us. A large round doily framed under glass hung on the wall above its rustic table. "What's this? It looks like…"

I got up and leaned into the other booth for a closer look. The sight of Mrs. Wilton's intricate stitching made my heart quicken. Her lacey work in fine ivory thread was displayed over a soft pink velvety background. Just like the lace-draped pink parlor with the piano and harp.

Two lines of embroidered script arched over the top of the doily with the words, "I praise you because I am fearfully and wonderfully made. All my days were written in your book before one came to be." And in the bottom right corner, a stitched signature read, Wilton.

A familiar voice behind me caught my attention.

"Welcome to *Café du Louvre*. I'm Cassie." There, greeting Dad and Hope, stood the same waitress who had served me in January. She saw me, and her eyes lit up. "Hi. I remember you." Then she noticed the framed doily and her eyes swept back to mine. "Wait, are you Penny?"

"What?" I was still tongue-tied over Mrs. Wilton's framed handiwork.

"A sweet elderly lady came in months ago and left this here. She said a young woman named Penny would be by to pick it up someday."

I stared at the framed doily again. It was true. Mrs. Wilton was real. Whether or not she was an angel, she was real. The waitress had seen her, and she had left this keepsake for me.

Cassie lifted the framed doily off the wall and I clasped it to my chest with joy before holding it out for Dad and Hope to see.

Hope took the picture as Dad scooted his chair over and wrapped an arm around my shoulder. "She knew you'd be back, looking for her."

I swiped away a tear at the corner of my eye. "And she must have known I'd wonder if she was real."

Hope laid the picture on the table and traced a fingertip over the wording. "It's so quaint, and what a sweet sentiment."

I leaned forward to study the stitches again. "It might be the same doily she was working on in January. I only wish you both could have gotten to know her."

We ate our lunch, complete with pie, though it wasn't because anything needed to be fixed. In fact, everything was just as it should be. Even the unknowns that lay ahead were not outside God's view. They were already written in His book.

Let the future come. I was safe in my Heavenly Father's hands.

A MESSAGE FROM THE AUTHOR

People often ask authors about the origins of their stories. They're curious to learn details about the process of bringing a book to life, and certainly these questions get a wide variety of responses.

Point Blank's origins are three decades old. Back then, it lingered as a solitary chapter tucked into a file folder along with a variety of other snippets of ideas that I hoped might one day find their way into my storytelling aspirations.

Eventually, as my publishing dreams got swallowed up by day-to-day life, that folder ended up in a box subsequently tucked away during one of our moves. It could have easily been pitched, but instead, it waited, unseen and nearly forgotten.

Though years passed, my dreams of writing never waned. When the time came that I felt ready to pursue a novel-length project, I didn't initially consider that folder of snippets, or even wonder where it had gone.

Fortunately, God always knew where that chapter was. He knew what sort of story should be developed from it. When the time was right, the folder came to light again, and I picked up the faded, typewritten pages and read Chapter One for the first time in at least a couple decades.

It still took a great deal of time and effort to complete Penny's story, of course. The plot didn't miraculously spring onto the page. I'm convinced, however, that the story you see today is one I could not have written all those many years ago. Not while I kept my own traumatic memories under lock and key.

I hope this story will encourage those who have experienced deep wounds and fears. For others, I hope they might get a glimpse into the Father-heart of God, who finds a way to put the right people and circumstances into place at the right time when we need them. Though this story is purely fiction, it was shaped as I considered how God had showed me his faithfulness in the midst of my own needs.

Here's the confidence I extend to you, dear reader: God has always known where you are. You've never been tucked away or forgotten. He has never lost track of his dreams and desires for your life and your future. You are much more than just a snippet of a life that might have been. You have a future and a hope (see *Jeremiah 29:11*).

My prayer is that readers might see how that theme has played out in Penny's story. How she took the steps that she could, and how her father completed what she was unable to do herself, and stood in the gap for her.

In spite of a separation that may seem impossible to mend, God is still watching for us and his son, Jesus, is still the Way, the Truth and the Life.

Blessings,

ACKNOWLEDGMENTS

No book is ever the work of one person. Any story planted in the heart and imagination of an author is shaped by a long process that involves input from many sources.

I'm greatly indebted to the American Christian Fiction Writers (ACFW) organization and especially my fellowship of local authors with the chapter in Colorado Springs. These marvelous people have provided a wealth of knowledge, and I've had the privilege of their consistent input and feedback while Penny's story took proper shape. My critique partners have been an essential part of this process, as well as beta readers and many others too numerous to mention individually.

Special thanks go to fellow author, Bryan Canter, who generously assisted with formatting the book's interior layout using his Vellum program. Thank you for saving me so many hours of tedious labor!

I'm grateful for the unwavering support of my

husband, Jim, who has not only been a faithful encourager, but a tireless supporter of so many of my creative endeavors over our more than four decades together. In the case of this particular story, he also served as a technical advisor with regard to law enforcement procedures and legal issues. What a wealth of information to have at my fingertips! I guess I'll have to keep you.

Likewise, my sister, Jan Harlow, provided tremendous assistance with some of the medical aspects of the story, helping to insure that Penny's dad and the hospital environment would be authentically portrayed. You spent precious time for me on this assignment—and in the midst of a global pandemic. A thank you seems hardly enough.

Most of all, I'm grateful to God, who gave me wonderful parents and a loving home to grow up in. In spite of the fact that I was initially religious out of a sense of obligation, He continually demonstrated His kindness toward me, ultimately guiding me to just the right place at just the right time, to discover the real depth of His amazing grace. I owe Him everything.

ABOUT THE AUTHOR

Diane M. Campbell has always been a daydreamer. As a child, she'd concoct far-away adventures while perched in the crook of a tree on her family's farm in rural Minnesota. Though tree-climbing has since been traded in for hammock-swinging, idle hours in the forest continue to be a source of inspiration for Diane's tales of mystery and adventure. It's no wonder the great outdoors is frequent setting in her stories.

She and her husband reside in Colorado where they enjoy spending their free time RVing and traversing remote mountain trails on their UTV.

In 2017, *Point Blank* received ACFW's (American Christian Fictions Writers) Genesis award for best suspense/thriller novel by a debuting author.

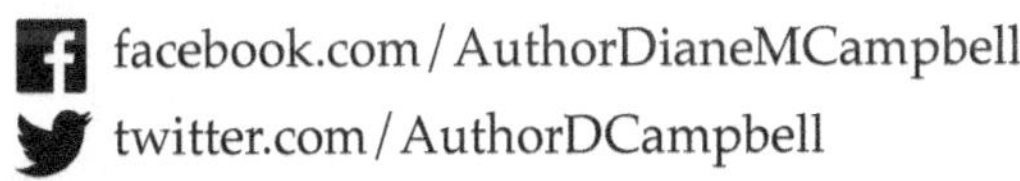

**Get all the latest updates on Diane's
writing endeavors by signing up
for her quarterly newsletter!**

As a thank you, she'll
send you this original
short story that
features Hope
McAllister, Penny's
quirky costume
accomplice
from Point Blank!

And how do
you sign up?

It's easy! Go to Diane's website (DianeMCampbell.net)
and look for the Newsletter Sign Up button on the
home page,
  –or–
scan this QR code and link
directly to the sign–up page!

You can also send an email via her website, or look for
her on Facebook and Twitter.
Diane loves to hear from readers!